ONE

The difficulty for Katie McGuire each day was to find a new place to cut. Both her inner thighs were scarred from years of cutting and although each laceration was little more than a nick, the cumulative effect was a mess. The trouble was that in the early days, when Katie first discovered this release, she hadn't had the reserve and self-control she now possessed. She had cut with the abandon of the explorer so early gashes were real gashes. These longer scars were still visible over twenty years later and Katie avoided cutting across them because it made her wince. Whether it really hurt more, she didn't know. There was a numbness in these old scars that meant her skin had lost its sense of touch (Wasn't that the point?), but it hurt her inside, in her tummy it seemed, and only on really bad days would she deliberately open old sores. But most days, and this was one of those days, just a little nick of a reminder would do.

First though, her bath – this was Katie's luxury, her indulgence and her peace. Katie set her alarm for six thirty in the morning. This was unnecessary because she woke immediately before the alarm went off but she let it be anyway. She used the radio alarm to catch the news because, although a lot of it was nonsense, it was essential she knew what nonsense was being spoken. There was a world out there and she was a part of it, a very real part of it – to the extent that she sometimes helped shape it – and the radio news was her first contact. At six thirty there were only the briefest of headlines but they were enough to bring her around before the inane music and DJ chatter took over until seven. News, weather – five minutes into Katie's day. What was to say how many things had already gone through her head? She slept well and enjoyed that slept-well feeling each morning. Her body felt good below the covers, not yet stirred into action but ready as soon as Katie gave the word.

She'd stopped seriously working out years before but did enough to maintain the hard-earned body of her youth. Of course, back then the gym was part of a crazy collective life that made exercise fun rather than a bore. When there's a whole crowd of you pushing each other on, when you know that all the other members hate you as they wonder how the owners ever let this crew join and is there a time when they're not here so that others might exercise in peace? And where do they get their money from: they never seem to work? Katie and her crowd must have seemed pretty intimidating to the other members, but they never gave it a second thought. They were never truly out of order, just loud and so obviously together, there being at times up to twenty of them, mostly fewer, but always three. Always three.

So Katie, who had a good body anyway – good as

in well looked after – no, not well looked after because already back then her abusive lifestyle was taking its toll, but good as in athletically fit and strong and at a weight suitable to her height – Katie gave her body a good grounding in those years that she would have had to go out of her way to lose in later life. Common sense in what she ate, walking to the station each morning and badminton once a week: these things kept her well, and this wellness was all she hoped for these days.

Was it important to her?

It was important she felt well for herself, and it was important she looked good for the world.

Katie explored her body as she lay in bed but never with her hands; she travelled her body with her mind. She'd taken what she could from yoga and enjoyed the relaxation technique of concentrating first on one part of her body and then on the next. Toes, feet and ankles; what did they mean by 'feel your ankles'? Imaginary feelings? Imaginary bullshit? Maybe, but she continued up to her calves, her shins and her knees. Yes, she liked these parts of her body; she knew her body was what would be regarded as beautiful. She skipped over her thighs. Her hips, her tummy, her shoulders and arms – strong arms, she'd always liked her arms – taking her time over her hands and fingers, touching each of her fingertips with each of her thumbs.

Enough for now, it was time to move. Ten minutes gone – if she ran her bath now she could be lying in it, clean and relaxed by the time for the news proper. She pushed back the covers and stood on the hard wood floor, stretched her hands to the ceiling and felt again the strength in each of her limbs.

Cats have it right, she thought.

She walked through to the bathroom, still in her pyjamas. Although it was officially spring – well, official to Katie, who went by the equinox; she'd never really got to grips with the Irish definition of when the seasons started and finished, mainly because she just dismissed it as wrong – there was a distinct chill in the air. Katie used a storage heater to warm the apartment through in the evening, plus a peat fire when she really felt the need, but she never set the timer for the morning, preferring a fresh start to the day rather than a muggy heat. She knew it wouldn't be to everybody's taste, but then what would she care about that? This wasn't some economy drive – there was never any shortage of hot water, always plenty of hot water – just a preference, possibly from her child-hood, when mornings in the house were a lot colder than now.

She leant over the bath to the taps, turning on the hot water and placing the plug in the bath. Requirement number one when looking for this apart-ment, for any apartment, was the bath. A good shower was a beautiful thing, and sometimes only a shower would do, but in the morning Katie had to have her bath. Even this simple turning on of the hot tap and hearing the water flow, a sound so familiar and commonplace, did something for Katie each day and she always took a second or two to let it register, to let it wash over her. She could live without it – she could live without anything, this she knew for a fact – but while she had the choice, she chose not to live without her bath.

She straightened to a standing position and looked at her face in the cabinet mirror, the briefest of glances that signified, what – maybe nothing? She left the bathroom, the water still running into the bath, and went on through to her living room/kitchen. She took the water filter jug from the fridge and poured enough to fill the cup she took from the drainer. She then poured the water from the cup into a pan standing on the cooker hob, turning on the heat and replacing the lid on the pan. The water jug she refilled from the tap and returned to the fridge. She took a chamomile teabag from a box in the cupboard – the press, she thought, the press – placed the teabag in the cup and then it was back into the living area for more yoga, again customized to her own needs.

She knelt in the middle of the floor with her back straight and her palms face down on her lap. She breathed through her nose as she accustomed herself to this position. On the third intake of breath she deliberately took in more air and tried to direct the air to her stomach. She was aware of the stupidity of this – naturally the air went to her lungs – but she tried none the less to let the air expand her stomach and her stomach only. She also tried to regulate her breathing and slow it down, taking deeper and longer breaths. When she felt she had mastered this – only a matter of about thirty seconds or so – she further extended the intake of breath and allowed the air first to her stomach and then up into her chest. She tried to imagine the motion of the air as a wave on the seashore, flowing in and flowing out of her body. The simple suggestion of a wave had stuck in her mind for many years now, and would probably stay with her for the rest of her life.

What was she thinking? That good posture was as important as they claimed? Or that breathing from the stomach really did work; that it had a calming effect, and if it worked here it would work in more stressful situations?

The water in the pan was about to come to the boil and the bath was just about run. On her final deep breath Katie opened her arms to the side, raised them up above her head and brought the palms of her hands together, holding the breath as she held the position before letting out the air and letting down her arms. She stood and returned to the kitchen, turning off the heat and pouring the water into the cup with the teabag.

In the bathroom Katie caught the hot water before it ran cold. There was just enough space to add some cooler water but Katie didn't bother – she liked her bath water hot, hotter than most people could tolerate, and she had her thermostat set at exactly that temperature. She took off her pyjamas and hung them on the handle of the bathroom door. She stepped into the bath water and, as ever, the temperature made her gasp. All her measured breathing from the yoga was replaced by short intakes of breath as she tried to accustom her body to the heat. First one foot and then the other; this was the easy part. Before she had a chance to reconsider, she grabbed the handles at the side of the bath and lowered herself to a sitting position. The sensation was close to deliberately scalding herself with boiling water, as if she'd poured in the water directly from the pan, but she forced herself to slide further down in the bath so her whole body was immersed in the water. She could feel the blood ringing in her ears and she knew this wasn't good for her body but, in a way that she couldn't explain, it was right for her.

She'd heard once about a girl who bathed each day in a solution of bleach and cold water – part of a never-ending need for cleanliness – and Katie knew she was not so different herself. Her heart went out to the girl even though they'd never met because Katie understood the compulsion to do that every day. For Katie, though, it wasn't the cleanliness and it wasn't the pain – it was the oblivion. Whatever else might happen to her during the day, whoever she might meet and whatever she might do, this moment of complete aloneness was the closest the world would ever see of the real Katie McGuire.

Katie's body became gradually accustomed to the temperature of the water. She was conscious of time passing, and she listened to the news headlines as they were read out on the radio. This was followed by a review of the day's papers and, when she heard the more in-depth news analysis, Katie knew it was time to move. She washed herself and stood in the bath. She pulled out the plug and the water began to drain away. She reached across for a towel and gently dabbed at her wet body; her skin was inflamed with the heat of the bath water and felt tender to the touch of the towel. She wiped away the condensation from the bathroom mirror and looked at herself properly for the first time that day. She challenged her reflection, forcing herself to look at her blotched skin.

'Not so beautiful now, are we?' she asked her reflection. Katie felt this conflict every day, between how the world perceived her beauty and how she believed herself to be.

She stepped out of the bath before the water had completely drained away and sat on the bathroom chair. For the first and only time that day she examined the scars along her inner thighs. She reached across to the shelf below the cabinet for a packet of flat, open razor blades, the type that used to be fitted onto safety razors with a screw. Each blade was individually wrapped in a paper envelope and Katie picked one out before returning the outer packet to the shelf. She unwrapped the blade and with absolutely no hesitation she cut into the skin of her thigh.

'You have to stay ugly,' she said quietly.

She replaced the blade in the wrapper and threw it into the bin – truly, a disposable razor. She reached for a packet of cotton pads and dabbed one onto the cut to stop the flow of blood. She held the pad with her fingers and then, as she stood, pushed her legs together to keep it in place.

Time was pressing now. If she was honest with herself, plucking her eyebrows took the best part of ten minutes each morning. She refused to set the alarm any earlier though, or to change her routine just to give herself longer on her face, despite the fact that she always ending up rushing out the door. She kept her make-up to a minimum, but this no-effort look was becoming harder to maintain each morning. She brushed her hair and tied it back, away from her face. Before leaving the bathroom, she let the pad fall away from the skin between her legs. She put it into the bin along with the razor blade and went through to the bedroom to dress.

No one would ever know because no one would ever need to know.

Her clothes at least gave Katie no grief in the morning. She'd adopted a look years ago – smart, business, professional – and had kept to it ever since. It wasn't exactly sexless because however hard she tried Katie couldn't completely conceal what was so obviously a part of her, but it was more or less what you'd expect a male investment banker to wear – only on a woman. For the first few years in this job, Katie had always worn trousers, both for practical purposes and also as part of the fight for the right to wear them at work. But as dress codes changed and Katie became both more confident and more senior, she also relaxed enough to wear the occasional skirt. She prepared all her clothes for the week on the preceding Sunday, so each morning it was a simple matter of dressing for the day.

She aimed to be out the door by seven thirty but always found she was sitting drinking her tea at this time, writing out her private list for the day. Some of the items featured on the list day after day, and were copied out from the previous day's list. So, for example, exercise and diet were the first two items each day; diet as in to maintain a healthy diet, not a diet to lose weight. These items were meant as a reminder to Katie to be conscious of her health and to take care with how she lived her life. If she could keep a check on her intake of fruit, salad and vegetables it was a reliable way of looking after her body. Other regular items on the list were her evening engagements, such as badminton or the cinema. She preferred to do activities like this straight from work – especially if they were on in town – rather than come home and then go out again. She liked her sleep, particularly during the week while she was working – so different to the old days – but she had nothing planned for this evening except a little shopping for a few basic groceries. She wrote these down to the right of her sheet of notepaper.

Katie's tea was now cool enough to drink. She

fetched her coat from the bedroom and switched off everything that needed to be switched off. She checked the time, which was now seven thirty-seven, put on her coat and went out the door. Her apartment was one of only two on this floor; there was a French couple living in the door opposite to her own, but they kept different hours to Katie and she rarely saw them. This was just how Katie liked it – she liked knowing they were there and they seemed really nice but they didn't need Katie and she didn't need them.

She had a woolly hat in her pocket that she put on her head when she felt the cold morning air. She wasn't concerned with how it made her look; keeping warm was much more important – that and the fact that her hat bore no label or logo. It was a brisk ten-minute walk to the DART station each morning, and the thought of missing her train encouraged Katie to step out briskly. She didn't want to wait in the cold and the carriages on the next train would be so much fuller and uncomfortable. There were a few other regular walkers from the estate – a lovely, private collection of apartments set in their own grounds – and Katie could judge if she was on time or slightly late by whom she saw. She knew this was nonsense because the other residents could be as late as she was, but no matter. She enjoyed the walk each day and it was only ever spoiled by heavy rain and wind; then she wished she had a car to keep her dry. On days like today, though, she felt oh so superior to all the lazy bastards who drove to the station.

Katie's fellow walkers were the first test of her anonymity. She loved the fact that what mattered most was the speed at which she walked – should she pass by this guy on the pavement in front, or slow down slightly, or cross over to the other side of the street? Were they both in good time for the train, and, if so, why was that woman running into the station? These people had no idea about the private Katie back in her apartment, and they never would have. There was nothing she wanted to know about them, and there was nothing they would ever know about her – except, of course, that she liked to catch the seven forty-five train in the morning.

Naturally, there were the same faces each morning on the station platform, but Katie had found this wherever she lived. More often than not, she wasn't waiting long enough at the station to let it bother her. She could see the light of the train coming towards her along the track. She chose not to buy a newspaper from the kiosk – trying to read on the train wasn't always a pleasure and besides there was no shortage of newspapers at work. She preferred to use the time of the journey – just over twenty minutes or so – to let her mind wander. If she concentrated on anything, it was on her breathing.

Katie looked up at the route plan for the DART above the carriage window and smiled. The stations were laid out on a single straight line, much like the various lines on the London Underground. Twice every working day, Katie was reminded of a set of questions she'd seen years ago on *University Challenge*. The route maps of three metro systems in Europe were shown in outline on the screen, and the contestants had to guess the city from the map. While none of the featured cities had quite as extensive a network as London, they all had more than a single track. Dublin's DART system would seem like a branch line for these other cities – something like the track from Newcastle to Whitley Bay – and not what you'd expect from a country's capital city. If you were being kind, you could add in the new Luas tram system, but it wasn't as though the trains and the trams were interconnected in any meaningful way.

And still no rail connection to the airport, thought Katie.

When she included this observation in her weekly column for the *Sunday Independent*, the response was fairly predictable. First there was the 'Well, if you don't like our country then you can fuck off back to where you came from' reaction; and second there was the 'It's our city and we know it's not perfect but we love it anyway.'

Katie's reply in her next article was to point out that she, at least, had chosen to live in this country and hadn't just happened to be born here. As such she was in a better position to compare Ireland with other countries and therefore have a much more informed opinion than the racist pricks who felt threatened every time their country was criticized. She also added that she was passing on the more extreme letters to the Gardaí for incitement to racial hatred. The second group of detractors – the Dubs who were so proud of their city – Katie insisted were part of the problem. If Dubliners couldn't see how the rest of the world saw Dublin, then nothing would ever change.

'Dubliners are like Scousers,' she wrote, 'and you can take that for the insult I mean it to be. You've fallen for the myths surrounding your city, and this stops you seeing how dirty and unsafe it really is. You believe that Dublin is the best city in the world, while the rest of us know it's a dump. You talk about a hundred thousand welcomes, but then you stick a knife in any foreigner you don't like. You say the *craic* is mighty, but only if you're white. And you think you're loved by everybody but, well, have I got news for you!'

So, of course, there was a whole new round of correspondence asking Katie just who was the racist now? To which Katie replied that if they were really interested in racism, they should take a Dublin taxicab ride – nine times out of ten they'd strike lucky.

'Nobody is addressing what I'm saying – that Dublin doesn't work as a city. It doesn't function well; it's dirty, and it's unwelcoming. Try walking the length of O'Connell Street – Dublin's Champs-Élysées! Or try waiting as a pedestrian to cross O'Connell bridge – this is not a safe city. And Ireland's capital shitty has no striking features to take your breath away. You can pay at the Guinness Hop Store to look out over the city skyline, but there's nothing there to see. So please don't be offended by what I have to say – just do something about it. After all, you keep saying it's your city.'

This provocative style was why the *Independent* asked Katie to write in the first place. She had originally written a letter to the *Irish Times*, asking why Ireland should be such an expensive place to live – what were the benefits; where was the pay-off? Other expensive countries could point to an excellent system of social welfare or a superior standard of living – what did we get for our money in Ireland?

The letter was printed on a day that Katie attended a training seminar at the Irish Management Institute.

'Is that you?' asked the woman in the seat next to Katie.

'I'm afraid so,' said Katie, and smiled.

The woman was a features editor at the *Sunday Independent* and was delighted to learn that Katie worked as an account manager in the Financial Services Centre. Over dinner that evening, she asked Katie to expand her letter into a full-length article.

Katie's article – 'What does that have to do with the price of fish?' – caused the kind of stir that newspapers like, and also turned Katie into something of a celebrity. The normally reserved and hidden world of investment banking was suddenly news because a young, successful and good-looking woman had dared to question the government's economic policy – what's more, she'd done so with a rigour and authority that made people smile. Katie was asked to write on a regular basis, but she initially declined.

'I'm not sure I have anything else to say,' she told the features editor.

But of course she did, and Katie was soon contributing a weekly column to the paper. She broadened her subject matter – it was hard to be consistently entertaining about economic policy – and more often than not it was the failings of Ireland's infrastructure that she wrote about.

'What's the point in digging a tunnel if you don't go under the river? It's one of the most perverse ideas I've ever heard. They claim they're going to take all this heavy traffic out of the city centre, but to where? Are all the truck drivers for Galway and Cork really going to head north in a tunnel to the car park they call the M50? So they can queue and pay a toll for the bridge across the river?'

Katie was bemused by the absurdity of modern life in Ireland. Her column was an irritant to the government, and being a thorn in its side is what made Katie such a success.

'My friends in England often ask me how the health care system works in Ireland. I tell them we pay a social insurance levy as they do in England but also pay each time we visit the doctor – they don't believe me.'

Katie enjoyed the provocation, especially when she forced readers to reveal it was her Englishness they couldn't handle, and not her argument. For the most part she believed her own rhetoric; she really did care and behind everything she wrote was a genuine concern for life in Ireland to be better.

'Would it be too difficult to hold a national debate – say, every two years – on the percentage allocation of government spending? Wouldn't it be nice to specify where our money goes? My guess is that government jets and new ministerial buildings wouldn't make the cut. Having a say would ease the pain of handing the money over in the first place and, who knows, perhaps it would make the government feel more accountable? Let's get away from this silly idea that the Minister for Finance is somehow better qualified than we are on how to spend our money.'

During her first TV appearance, she referred twice to Bob Geldof's reason for leaving Ireland in the seventies – he couldn't stand the mediocrity – and Katie claimed that nothing much had changed. And yet she still chose to live in Ireland; this, for Katie, was the proof of her sincerity.

It was appearing on television that transformed Katie into a national figure; writing for the *Independent* was all well and good, but television made her name. On the one hand there was this tough, sexy babe, not afraid of using her looks to unnerve the men in suits across from her. You could see how Katie disarmed them – try as they might, they couldn't resist letting slip the occasional 'good girl', and it was then that Katie moved in for the kill. She dismantled her opponents' arguments and left them for dead. They knew they'd been had but it was too late; they'd been made to look like gombeens on national television.

(Just as once in a mixed badminton match, Katie's

male opponent had complained that she'd deliberately not worn a bra to distract him. There was no way he could win his argument; he looked like a lech and Katie still won the game.)

So here was Katie, who valued her privacy and yet wrote for a national newspaper; who had more reason than most to keep herself to herself and yet appeared on national television. These were just the extreme examples of the contradiction in Katie's working life; simply stepping outside her front door was enough to set the contradiction in motion for the day. Her fellow commuters didn't know her; her work colleagues didn't know her; and the readers of her newspaper column didn't know her – they were all just different points on the same scale. A long time ago, she had a choice – whether to stay at home or to go out into the world – and this was her way of living with that choice.

The journey into town gave Katie a further opportunity to prepare for the day ahead. By the time the train arrived at Connolly Station, she had become the public persona she projected. It was a short walk to Katie's office – a huge building shared by several companies – and she deliberately slowed her pace for this final leg of her commute. She hated turning up to work hot and bothered from walking too fast and, besides, there was no need; she was in good time. It was an easy trip each day, all things considered; the only way it could have been easier was if she chose to live in the city centre, but she preferred the remove of Monkstown.

Katie showed her pass to Charlie the security guard.

This wasn't really necessary – it was the scanning of the bar code that let her in – but Charlie had been a fixture on the door from long before Katie's time, and knew most of what went on in the building.

'Good morning, Charlie,' said Katie, and pushed through the barrier.

'Good morning to you, Ms Katie McGuire,' he replied. 'At it again in yesterday's paper, I see.' Yesterday's *Independent* was on the counter, next to Charlie's elbow and a half-drunk mug of tea.

'And what do you think?' asked Katie. 'Did I over-step the mark this time?'

'No more than usual, I'd say, no more than usual.'

Charlie smiled and smoothed down the hair on his scalp.

'Oh well,' said Katie, 'give the punters what they want, eh?'

'What you have to say isn't always what they want.'

'They love it,' said Katie, 'and you know they do.'

Katie could feel Charlie's eyes on her as she walked over to the lift. She guessed he shook his head each day at the waste – Charlie wasn't alone in presuming that Katie was a lesbian, but if that was what it took then that was fine by Katie. She recognized a couple of the people waiting for the lift, but she didn't know anyone to speak to. Katie worked on the fourth floor. Open-plan desk arrangements fanned out from the central lift shaft in a huge expanse of space with private offices lining the outer walls. It wasn't exactly a trading floor, more like somebody's idea of one.

Katie walked the length of the room to her office, and called out her good mornings to the few colleagues already at their desks. She knew she looked like Sigourney Weaver in the film *Working Girl* – all business and ready for the day, striding across the floor – but only because Carmel, her assistant, her Melanie Griffith, wouldn't ever let her forget it.

'Good morning, Ms Boney-Ass,' said Carmel. She switched off her mobile and dropped it into her bag.

'Good morning, Carmel,' said Katie, and smiled. 'How's the world of Mergers and Acquisitions? Was that Harrison Ford you were just speaking to?'

'You might laugh,' said Carmel, 'but one day you'll find it's this girl sat in that office of yours, and not that sorry bag of bones you call a behind.'

'Harrison might like my bottom.'

'No,' said Carmel, 'he's going to want something to get a hold of, something to sink his teeth into – and I think I'm just his type.'

'Steady, girl.' Katie laughed. 'Steady.'

The call from Mike came through at three minutes past nine, as though he considered nine o'clock the acceptable time to ring. Katie took no calls before ten thirty unless Carmel considered it absolutely necessary. Add on the three minutes of Carmel refusing to put Mike through, and you have three minutes into some people's working day – but not that many people anymore. Katie looked from the phone to the clock and lifted the receiver.

'Carmel?'

'I'm sorry, Katie,' said Carmel, 'but he won't go away.'

'Who is it?'

'That's just it, he won't say; he just keeps repeating that it's imperative he talks only to you. He says he's a close personal friend.' The conviction drained out of Carmel's voice. 'He's very nice,' she added as an after-thought.

Katie smiled. It was obviously absurd to Carmel that Katie should have a close personal friend.

'What do you think?' she asked. 'Should I take the call?'

'I think he'd better wait like all the others,' said Carmel.

'Niceness just doesn't cut it, really, does it?'

'It does no harm,' said Carmel, 'but it's not enough to get put through to you. I'll ask him to call back later.'

Katie replaced the receiver and returned to her newspaper. She'd established this right – to read through the papers each morning before actually doing what was recognizably her job – only by being year after year the best performing account manager in the company. She was disdainful of her colleagues' cursory glance at the newspapers; they only looked at the business pages, as though this justified the wasted time. She had no patience with anyone who claimed to read the paper each day, when – surprise, surprise – if she referred to something she'd seen, it was always that one particular article they hadn't read. So much so that Katie occasionally asked certain colleagues if they'd seen such-and-such a piece, just out of bloody-mindedness, and guess what? The results were not encouraging. Katie's record stood for itself – if she preferred to start her day with a review of the news-papers, the company wasn't about to lose her over something so trivial. Katie likened it to all the top man-agement gurus agreeing that a few minutes' medita-tion in the workplace produced measurable results. Very few managers could tolerate the sight of an employee just sat at their desk, apparently doing nothing. As though the employee should put up a sign – 'Meditating, now fuck off!'

Newspapers helped Katie to manage other people's money, but they also kept her sharp as a person; she was never short of something to talk about, either professionally or socially. And there were so many different types of news – the broadsheets, the tabloids, plus the TV screens outside in the main office, and there was Carmel, a compulsive listener to the radio and a constant source of information. Katie loved it all, loved it all in itself and not just for its application to her job.

This ability to soak up and analyse information from so many different sources was part of what made Katie such a good account manager. She thought very little about buying stock as she read through the papers. She wasn't certain there was a direct relationship between the two but, if she didn't know at least something of what was happening in the world, she would have been less able to make the decisions she took on a daily basis.

She also knew that an hour rarely made that much difference to the financial markets; there was always plenty of time for studying figures on a computer screen. Katie had made her name by saying it was okay to do nothing if that was what the markets required; when the markets demanded it, the newspapers were dumped immediately.

The crazy thing was that soon everybody who reported directly to Katie thought it best to conscientiously study the papers each morning. It was weird to come out her office for a coffee break and find a floor full of bankers with newspapers spread out on their desks. So much so, she had to persuade them this wasn't absolutely necessary.

'If you want to read the papers, you can,' she said. 'But if you don't feel the need, don't just do it for the sake of it.'

Organizations, she thought, and the people in them. When asked how she consistently achieved such good results – whether by her superiors, her colleagues or, occasionally, the press – she had one piece of advice: always buy undervalued stock. It was simple, too simple for some people, but it was the one thing she insisted upon amongst her own team.

'Never forget this is someone else's money – it doesn't even belong to the bank. We're gambling with other people's money, but you should behave as though it were your own. The bank pays you money to make more money with other people's money; if you do that then everybody will be happy.'

Of course this wasn't the whole story but it was as good a basis as any for a young trader to start out on. Katie's department was traditionally the company's training ground for new employees. She much preferred a team of raw recruits to the older, more experienced hands; it was fun and it kept Katie on her toes.

Soon after ten each day, Katie took her coffee break with Carmel in the staff canteen. This was her real breakfast time, her favourite meal of the day, and nothing – nothing! – came between Katie and her coffee. She walked through and made a silent drinking-from-a-cup gesture to Carmel.

Carmel was on the phone, as usual. She took the receiver away from her ear and pointed at the mouth-piece.

'What?' asked Katie.

Carmel covered the receiver with her hand.

'It's him,' she said. 'He's still on the line.'

'Who?'

Carmel spoke into the phone.

'I'm just putting you on hold again,' she said, and pressed a button on the phone. 'The guy from before – he wouldn't hang up; said he preferred to wait. This guy really wants to speak to you.'

'That was over an hour ago,' said Katie.

'I know, but what could I do?'

'Hang up on him, maybe? Have you been speaking to him all this time?'

Carmel blushed.

'I told you, he's really nice.'

'But an hour, Carmel – what have you been talking about? On second thoughts, forget it – I don't want to know. Come on; let's go for coffee. If he's still there when we come back, I'll speak to him then.'

'He says his name's Mike,' said Carmel. 'He said to tell you that it's Nice Guy Mike; that you'd know who I mean.'

Katie looked at Carmel.

'Nice Guy Mike – he said that?'

'Yes,' said Carmel. 'Do you know who he is?'

'What did he tell you?' asked Katie. She heard the harsh tone in her own voice and corrected it. 'I mean, did he tell you why he's calling?'

'Not really, he just told me his name.'

'In an hour?'

'Well . . . we mostly talked about me. What do you want me to do?'

Katie leant her weight against Carmel's desk and breathed in deeply through her nose.

'I don't know anyone by that name,' she said.

'He said you'd say that.'

'I'd remember anyone calling himself Nice Guy Mike.'

'He said you'd say that too,' said Carmel. 'And that you'd ask for his surname, but that you know it already and know why he can't give it.'

Katie looked at the receiver in Carmel's hand.

'If he – if it is who he says it is, ask him to call back in half an hour. There's no need for him to keep holding on; tell him I'll take his call.'

'He won't believe me. He won't hang up.'

'Tell him – tell him if he doesn't hang up I won't speak to him. Tell him that, and then you hang up.'

Katie's young team tended to share the same table for their break each morning. A few people sat alone with a book or a newspaper, but mostly it was an opportunity to chat or joke or flirt. The canteen was shared by the whole building, and there was a loud buzz of conversation among the different groups of employees.

Katie was unusually quiet. Even when the talk turned to one of her pet subjects – the crappiness of most TV advertising – she appeared distracted and oblivious to the banter at the table.

'I think the worst one I've seen recently,' said Carmel, 'has to be the ad – they're a department store, I think – that ends up by claiming that they're "almost nation-wide". I mean, if you're not completely nationwide, you don't mention it, do you? It's like saying – we know what we're doing, almost, but not quite.' She spoke across Katie to Ronnie, a recent arrival at the company and one of Katie's protégés.

'I disagree,' said Ronnie. 'The worst one by far has to be for Irish Rail. You know, where they reel off how many more carriages they're running on each line, and then hit us with the punchline – "And more to follow".'

'Yes.' Carmel laughed. 'Like they're proud of something they haven't even done yet, and want to tell the world.'

'Somebody, somewhere,' said Ronnie, 'decided they should run with that ad.'

'An advertising executive,' said Carmel, 'or a room full of advertising executives.'

'Er yeah,' said Ronnie, 'right, so we're all agreed then? We'll run with the "more to follow" promise?'

'More to follow – almost nationwide,' said Carmel.

Katie was pleased to see Ronnie confident and relaxed at the table – the likes of Carmel were quite intimidating if you didn't know them – but she couldn't bring herself to join in. A subject like this was often enough for a few Katie McGuire gems, but not today; she smiled along, but was happy for the coffee break to be over. She took the lift and walked back to the office with Carmel.

'Are you mad at me over that phone call?' Carmel was used to Katie being frank with her; if she was in trouble she wanted to know.

'What – no,' said Katie and walked on.

'Then what the fuck is it?' asked Carmel, and stopped by her desk.

Katie looked up at Carmel.

'Sorry, I . . .'

'Are you okay? You don't look too good – is it that Mike?'

'No, no – it's fine. I'm fine.'

'I can get rid of him, if that's what you want.'

'No, really, thanks. I'm fine. Put him through when he calls. I'm sorry if I was being rude. It's just . . .'

'A surprise to hear from him?'

'Yes, you could say that.'

'Well, as I said – he seems nice.'

Katie smiled. 'Oh yes,' she said. 'He's that all right.'

Carmel's phone rang. Katie looked up at the time; it was exactly ten thirty.

'You'd best put him through,' she said to Carmel. She walked into her office and closed the door.

'Mike?'

'Katie, how are you? Thanks for taking my call.'

'I had to – if only to get my assistant to do some work today.'

'I'm sorry about that. I thought if I let her go I'd never get through to speak to you. Would you apologize to Carmel on my behalf?'

Katie could hear the nervousness in Mike's voice.

'On your behalf? Yes, I'll apologize to Carmel on your behalf. Why are you calling, Mike?'

'Well,' he said, 'I'm here in Dublin today, and I thought we might meet up – if you'd like to, that is.'

'We agreed never to contact each other again,' she said. 'Under any circumstances – do you remember? So why are you calling me?'

'But that was such a long time ago,' said Mike. 'And I'm in Dublin so rarely these days. I saw your column in the paper yesterday – it's very good, you know – and I thought, well, why not? You're such a public figure now, what harm could it do to get in touch?'

'Cut the crap, Mike! I want to know why you called. We had an agreement and you just broke it – why?'

Katie knew how easy it was to get sucked into Mike's

pleasantries; she knew how overwhelming they could be.

'But, Katie,' he said, 'does all that really matter any more?'

'I asked you a question,' said Katie. 'If you're not going to be straight with me then I'm hanging up, and you won't be put through again. You have one minute to explain why you called before I put down the phone.'

'Katie – '

'One minute, Mike.'

Katie watched the second hand tick around the face of the clock on her wall. A minute wasn't long enough to get a grip on hearing Mike's voice again, not long enough to come to terms with Mike getting back in touch. The very mention of his name – Nice Guy Mike – upset her, and Katie could feel her defences crumbling, defences she'd spent half a lifetime creating. It was a shock rather than a surprise, because she feared the past coming back into her present. She was scared of what that past might drag along with it. If she let in the past, she let in worry and anxiety, she let in guilt and regret, and, if she was honest with herself, she let in loneliness. So she used the minute's silence to reconstruct the barriers in her mind. She breathed deeply and deliberately.

'Katie.'

Mike spoke exactly on the minute, if only to stop Katie putting down the phone.

'Why did you call?' she asked. More silence. 'Mike?'

'I'm in trouble, Katie. I'm in trouble, and I need your help.'

'We agreed never to contact each other,' repeated Katie.

'I know, but – '

'We agreed for this very reason – that if either of us was in trouble, we wouldn't drag each other down. And now you're here, phoning me at my workplace; you're setting up a connection, a lead, from you to me. Where are you calling from?'

'From a public phone box, in the lobby of a hotel.'

'Where people can hear you?'

'No, it's quiet.'

'And you were using that same phone to speak to Carmel? How did you pay for the call? You weren't pumping coins into the slot for an hour – your credit card?'

Mike didn't reply.

'Are you fucking stupid, Mike? I'm putting down the phone – don't call me again.'

'Don't go, Katie, please – I need your help.'

'You never needed anyone's help, Mike, least of all mine. Whatever you're playing at, I'm not interested. These are the exact circumstances in which you – you, Mike – said not to call. This was your rule and you made me swear to it. God knows there were times . . . I could have tracked you down because I needed you, but I didn't. And now you're doing what we swore we'd never do, and knowing you, Mike, knowing you, there's another reason behind this and I don't want to know.'

'You don't take much tracking down,' said Mike. 'All I have to do is open the newspaper and you're there.'

'That doesn't give you the right to contact me; it doesn't mean all bets are off. Maybe I thought it safer to keep a high profile. What isn't safe is for you to call me at the first sign of trouble.'

'I received a letter from the FBI,' said Mike.

'What?'

'The FBI. They wrote to me, telling me I'd be receiving a subpoena to appear in a US court of law.'

'Bullshit!'

'Bullshit or not, they know who I am.'

'Counting cards in Vegas isn't a crime,' said Katie.

'You know as well as I do this isn't about counting cards in Vegas. I'm a US citizen, remember; I could end up doing a serious amount of time in prison.'

'Yeah, but you're also a British citizen – and an Irish one too, come to that – I can't imagine them prosecuting you.'

'They don't like being made fools of,' said Mike.

'It was over twenty years ago; they're hardly going to pursue you after all this time.'

'But they are doing, aren't they? We fucked them over and they don't like it. And what I hear about US prisons, I don't much like either.'

'You're not going to prison, Mike.'

'We messed with their precious system, and we cheated them out of their money. There's nothing they care more about than their money.'

'But it wasn't even that much,' said Katie. 'I mean,

it was a lot of money at the time, but by today's standards it was nothing.'

'We proved it could be done; that's what's pissing them off.'

'You proved it could be done,' corrected Katie. 'I just went along for the ride.'

'And the money,' said Mike.

'Yes, the money, but until you called there was no connection from me to that money. I'm not the one being subpoenaed.'

'I'm scared,' said Mike.

'Bullshit again,' said Katie. 'I don't know what it is you're up to, Mike but – '

'I'm not up to anything. I just need to see you; I need to talk to you.'

'You want to meet?'

'Yes, I'm in Dublin today, and I want to see you. I'm in the Gresham. I'll be here until three this afternoon. If you ask at reception, they'll let you know where to find me. I understand if you – '

'No,' said Katie. 'You can't do that, Mike. I have a life here; you can't just walk back into it and ask to see me again – not after twenty years.'

'I know how it must look, and I don't do it lightly – '

'I don't care how lightly you're doing it – the answer's no. I have too much to lose for it to be fucked up by you. I appreciate everything you did for me, Mike, but that was a long time ago and I can't go back there.'

'Please, Katie – '

'No! I'm going now, Mike, and I don't want you to call again.'

She put down the phone and looked at the receiver. She looked at the receiver for a long time. It didn't ring again until Carmel called through to remind Katie she had a meeting scheduled for eleven; everybody was waiting.

TWO

I

Katie first met Mike on the day she started college. She was twenty years old and nervous. She shuffled along in a line of law students, and waited to collect her timetable for the year. There was a lot of noise in the corridor – a lot of loud and anxious conversation. Everybody seemed to know everybody else, and Katie couldn't understand how. It didn't occur to her that they might be as nervous and as apprehensive as Katie was, and show it in a different way. All she saw was a confidence that bordered on arrogance; unlike Katie, they had every right to be there.

This was Katie's first real contact with a massed body of university students, and she wasn't too sure what to expect. The morning had been reassuringly anonymous – she registered with the university, was issued with a library card and directed to the bursar's office to pick up her grant. She did what was asked of her, and retreated to her flat in Hulme in Manchester for lunch. But the afternoon was different: this was her introduction to the Law Department. If she was determined to go through with this – and she was – she had to learn how to talk to these people. So she watched and listened and waited in line.

A desk was set up outside a lecture theatre. Three

employees from the Law Department – the secretary and two of her assistants – gave each student a seminar and lecture timetable, and directed them into the theatre. Katie had deliberately toned down her usual clothes – she wore her black combats, a plain top and her leather jacket – but she could see immediately that her appearance made the secretary uncomfortable. Katie had hacked her hair short with scissors before leaving for the college that morning; that might have been okay, but she also insisted on wearing an open razor blade on a chain around her neck. It was this that was freaking out the secretary.

'McGuire,' said Katie, as she stepped up to the desk. 'Katie McGuire.'

The student next to Katie looked up and smiled.

'Really?' he said. 'My name's Maguire.' He turned back to the secretary. 'Mike Maguire.'

The coincidence of the names was too much for the secretary to let go.

'Now what are the chances of that?' she asked, beaming. 'Out of all these people – you're not related, are you? No, you spell your names differently, I see.'

The other student held out his hand to Katie.

'I'm Mike,' he said. 'I'm an M-A-G Maguire; I take it you're an M-C-G?'

Katie saw the outstretched hand but didn't know what to do. Well, she knew she should shake his hand, but she didn't expect the boy to be so formally polite – it didn't seem a very student-like thing to do. And he was just a boy – Katie knew she was a year or two older than most first years, but this Mike looked to be about fifteen. Yet he had the assurance of a twenty-year-old that Katie could only wish for.

'How do you do?' he asked. He had an incredibly strong accent – so much so that even these few words were almost incomprehensible to Katie. What she heard was 'Hadjadae?' or 'Had your day?' And what had he said about her name? She reached for the timetable information from the secretary and walked away without saying a word. She went through to the lecture theatre and took the first seat she saw available.

Katie had never been in such a room before. She took in the tiered seating and the amphitheatre shape, and noticed how the shelf on which she rested her arms would double as a desk on which to make notes. The noise in here was even more intimidating. Everybody but Katie seemed to be talking to somebody. She looked around, but only caught the eye of Mike as he walked into the room. She quickly turned away, but Mike wasn't to be put off. He made his way over to Katie, and sat down next to her.

'I'm sorry,' he said. 'I didn't mean anything about your name. Maybe we can start over?'

'What,' snapped Katie, 'you think the way I spell my name says something about me – is that it?'

'No, I didn't mean – '

'I don't know about where you come from,' she said, 'but it means fuck all here,' she said.

'I'm sorry,' he repeated. 'I'm – '

But his politeness made Katie all the ruder.

'Listen,' she said. 'I can't understand a single fucking word you're saying, okay? So don't bother.'

'Oh,' he said. 'Oh,' and turned away.

Shit, thought Katie, what a great start. She didn't know what she'd expected, but it certainly wasn't this. And now she had to sit next to this guy for at least twenty minutes. There were just so many people here – it reminded her of school and that wasn't good. She closed her eyes in an attempt to shut out the noise – to shut out the memories of classrooms gone by – but this was never going to work.

Only when someone approached the podium down below did the room quieten down. A young female lecturer said a few words of welcome and gave a brief explanation of the difference in study methods now they were at university.

'This is perhaps the only time you'll all be here in the one place together,' she said. 'If you don't attend the lectures, no one will ever know but yourself – until, of course, it becomes obvious that you can't keep up with your coursework. Seminars and tutorials are a different matter and are compulsory; failure to attend means failure of the course.'

There had to be some doddery old lecturers somewhere within the Law Department, but for today at least they were being kept under wraps. The woman below was young enough to remember what it was like to be only starting out as an undergraduate.

'You'll receive no direction during the year in how to study,' she continued. 'If I have any advice to give you now, it's this: make the library your home, and read and learn every case history you can. The whole of English law is in those cases. From here on in it's up to you. How you get the reading done is up to you. How you get the essays in on time is up to you. You're on your own – so good luck.'

This suited Katie. She'd spent the past four years studying on her own, and now she'd signed up for four more. If today was unusual – an aberration – perhaps Katie could just keep her head down and do the work? But if it were like this every day she arrived for a lecture, she'd have to find a better way of coping. She'd handled today badly, and didn't want the next time to be so bad. It was one thing to keep a low profile, but quite another to attract attention to herself by being so obsessively private. She knew she'd been rude, and turned back to the guy sat next to her, to Mike.

'So many people,' she said. The noise and conversation started up again as the lecturer left the podium.

'Not for long,' said Mike.

'What do you mean?' asked Katie.

'Well, they deliberately start with too many students. If they have too large an intake, they can fail who they like throughout the year.'

'What do you mean?' asked Katie again.

'You heard what the woman said – they'll fail about a third of us before the first year is out.'

'But how do you know?' asked Katie. 'Why would they do that?'

'How many people are here?' asked Mike. 'About

three hundred – that's the number of places available on the course. And only two hundred graduate from this department every year. It's there in the maths.'

'But why?'

'So they can be sure of who they graduate. It's like a second recruitment process; it gets rid of anyone they think isn't up to the course.'

This was news to Katie and a shock; it must have shown on her face.

'Don't worry,' said Mike. 'I'm sure you'll be fine.'

Katie knew it would be hard at college, but she hadn't reckoned on such a high chance of failure. Having got there against the odds – studying alone, catching up on the years of lost schooling, applying for one of the toughest possible courses – it looked as though her battle wasn't over yet. And her first day hadn't been such a success. She just didn't know how to act with other people; she couldn't go through this every time she met someone new.

She cut herself badly that night.

Katie was right in thinking she could retain some anonymity while studying for her degree. The numbers attending the lectures were large, but she soon became used to that. Seminars were harder – Katie had to contribute in these smaller groups, or the tutor would notice and Katie would drop marks. It was in these early classes that Katie learnt the skills of argument – that when it came to the rules, there were no rules. First, she had to confront the snobbery she came across each day, imagined or otherwise. Katie brought a baggage of inferiority into the class, and felt that everybody talked down to her; she could take it from the tutors but not from the students. Then there was the intellectual intimidation, the assumption that surely she was aware of such and such a case – that what Katie was saying was nonsense. This happened twice before Katie realized that it wasn't snobbery, and it wasn't arrogance. Only one thing really mattered, and that was that she won her arguments. She played up her persona as the naive innocent or went on a charm offensive to disarm her classmates, and these worked for a while; but eventually Katie learnt to depend on her brains. It was, after all, what she did best.

There were many new accents that Katie had never heard before. They might have been easier to understand than Mike's, but for Katie they were just as strange. When it came to making friends, Katie remained distant to the point of being rude; if she was thought of badly, she'd rather that than get to know anyone or – and this would have been worse – allow anyone to get to know her. She knew from school that people needed to put you in a box, a category they could be comfortable with, and if Katie's category was 'difficult' then so be it. If she was to live out in the world, she wanted to do so on her own terms. The alternative was to give up and go back into care, this time as an adult, and that didn't appeal to her one little bit.

Katie had a flat on Bonsall Street in Hulme. It wasn't

unusual for students to live in Hulme – it was cheap and close to college – but it was strange for a first year, and unheard of for any student to live on her own. But she was well able to look after herself; she'd looked after her mother and aunt when she was only nine years old – her grandmother too for a while. She was discovered by the social services when she called a doctor to the house; she wanted to know what to do with the dead body of her grandmother. Until this age she hadn't attended school, or played with other children, or done anything really, other than cook and clean and skivvy for the adults in the house.

Katie was taken into care, and for the first time in her life she came into contact with other children. School was difficult. Katie never caught up with her studies – she deliberately and wilfully refused – and she carried the added stigma of living with people other than her parents. There were repeated attempts and failures to find her a foster home, but Katie resisted this as she resisted everything. She wore down a succession of social workers, and her teachers never looked beyond the legal requirement of Katie attending school. This lack of interest suited Katie; she knew what was expected of her – just like the teachers – and was quite happy just to go through the motions.

By the age of fourteen she had found enough privacy to do herself harm. The secrecy of cutting herself became the focus of her day – not an easy task when you're in care.

It was only when Katie was no longer legally obliged

to attend school – at the age of sixteen – that she recognized the use of an education. If you were unsympathetic, you could say she started to grow up, but Katie had done her fair share of growing up as a child. She realized that studying for and passing exams could change who she was; it might even eradicate where she came from, and help her choose whom she wanted to be. Qualifications were a ticket; she didn't know where that ticket might take her, but she knew she needed to be some place else.

Katie had to ask for help – again, not an easy thing when you've alienated just about everybody in your world. She learnt how to study independently, and was as bloody-minded and determined to catch up as she had once been not to learn. She spent a year discovering just how much she already knew; seven years of compulsory attendance at school had left its mark after all. The day centre she attended supported Katie's application to sit her O level examinations for the following year, the summer of 1977. The crisis the exams brought on, and the frenzy of cutting that followed, was Katie's real initiation into adulthood. She was faced with the stark consequences of her choice to better herself; she either did this thing or she accepted defeat, and gave in. She didn't give in, but it was hard not to.

Only Katie was surprised at how well she did in the exams, and it gave her the confidence to go on to take three A levels the following year. She also read a great deal for the first time in her life – studying *The Grapes of Wrath* for her English led Katie on to a succession of twentieth-century American writers. She loved *Gatsby*, and Holden Caulfield of course, but more than anything it was the fact that there was a whole world out there – or at least a whole continent – that was completely different to anything Katie had ever known. Like the books, America seemed accessible. The enormity of the landscape was appealing to her, and Katie realized just how limited a world she lived in.

Once Katie turned eighteen, she was free to live where she liked – or wherever the council would allocate her a flat. This was another huge step for her, but by now Katie had learnt to recognize the decisive moments for what they were. She was able to jump the queue on the housing list, though in truth there wasn't that much of a queue to live in Hulme; you had to be pretty desperate to want to live there – or a student, of course.

It soon occurred to Katie that she was clever enough to go on to college, if that was what she really wanted to do. She was too late to apply for that same year, immediately after taking her A levels, but her grades were such that she'd be accepted anywhere. There was no question of her leaving Manchester, and it was typical of Katie that she chose to study law. It was one of the hardest subjects to get into – as though Katie was deliberately putting it up to herself – but it made sense in other ways too. There was no A level she could have taken that would have particularly equipped her for a degree in law; even those applicants that had already studied law were told to forget everything they'd been taught and to start afresh. And if Katie was to sell herself as a model of self-improvement – and she could see in the interview to get on the course that this was what everyone wanted of her – what better subject than the law? Her social worker was happy, the university was happy, and she received an unconditional offer of a place to start in October of 1979. She was frustrated with the wait, and asked for a reading list well in advance.

Katie grew to like the mix of people around the flats. Hulme was very different to its more famous neighbour Moss Side, both racially and architecturally. A few terraced streets remained but Hulme was dominated by the crescents of flats, a nightmare vision of planning more suited to Ceaușescu's Romania than inner-city Manchester. Moss Side had an identity, whatever you thought of that identity; it was compact and defined. Hulme was a sprawling mess, with traces remaining of all the many failed attempts to provide housing that people could afford.

There were Irish pubs, there were black pubs and there were student pubs; there were pubs that managed to be all three at different times of the day or on different days of the week. There were families still around from when the flats were first built; there were business types who liked living close to town and paying so little rent; and there were untold numbers who had opted out – from work, from college, from what was left of society. There was a drug culture, but it was a laid-back drug culture; it was nobody's business but your own if you chose to get wasted. Katie wasn't stupid or careless; she was a woman, alone – a beautiful woman, alone, however hard she tried to hide it. There were times and places to avoid but generally she felt safe. She had a way of walking – invisible walking, she called it – ghosting through the streets at all hours, to and from the Law Library. She heard things at night-time but nothing like what she had heard as a little girl.

It was at most a ten-minute walk from Bonsall Street to the Law Library. Katie had heeded the young lecturer's advice and made the library her second home. She was happy to return to the discipline of studying. The Law Library was closer and convenient, with a much wider range of case law than either the John Rylands or the Central Reference Library in town. It was also possible to use it at any time, day or night, and Katie took full advantage. She had only herself to please. Once she knew her timetable, she adjusted her work-study and sleep accordingly. The library was naturally much quieter at night-time – though Katie was rarely alone – and sleeping through the day in Hulme wasn't unusual, it was the norm. By early November of that first term she had a steady routine that allowed her to follow the course without becoming at all involved in university life.

Katie was invisible walking along Oxford Road towards the library one night when she heard someone shout her name.

'Hey, McGuire.'

Katie hesitated for a second, and then walked on.

'Hey!'

She knew it was Mike from the day of registration. She remembered how badly she'd handled meeting him that day, and this made her stop and turn around. Mike held open the door of a black cab, and spoke instructions to whoever was inside.

'Stay there,' Katie heard Mike say, like he was training a dog. He left the cab and walked over to Katie.

'Where are you going?' he asked. 'It's Katie, isn't it? I'm Mike, remember, from the first day of term?'

'Yes,' said Katie. 'I remember.' She thought for a second that he might offer to shake her hand again, but Mike had obviously learnt.

'Where are you going?' he asked again.

'To the library,' said Katie.

'At this time? It's almost midnight.'

'It's quiet,' she said. 'I prefer it with fewer people around.'

'But what about sleep,' asked Mike, 'or recreation, and fun – things like that?' He grinned at Katie.

'Which are you about to do,' she asked, 'sleep or recreation? Your friends are looking for you, by the way.'

Two students were stepping out from the cab onto the pavement.

'No,' shouted Mike. 'Eugene, Rory – get back in the cab. Just wait in the cab. I'm coming now, okay? Don't let the cab leave, whatever you do.'

But it was too late. One or the other, Eugene or

Rory, reacted to something the driver said, and closed the door of the cab. The two of them stood and watched as the taxi drove away.

'Oh Jesus,' said Mike to Katie, 'this is harder than I thought it was going to be.' He called over to his friends again. 'Look, just stand there, okay? We still have to wait for Bruno. Just stand still and don't move.' He turned back to Katie and smiled. 'Mathematicians,' he said. 'They don't get out too often.'

'But they're out with you tonight?'

'Something like that, yes. We're going to the casino.'

'The casino?' asked Katie. 'How old are you?' As soon as she said it, she regretted it.

'Eighteen,' said Mike. 'Well, almost, anyway. Rory tells me – I know Rory from home – Rory tells me Eugene has something wonderful to show us.'

'At the casino?'

'It's to do with playing cards – blackjack, actually.'

'And where's home?' asked Katie.

'Belfast,' said Mike. 'Can you understand what I'm saying yet?'

'Barely,' said Katie. 'I thought you were Scottish.' She was still ashamed of how she'd behaved when they first met. 'I've never been out of Manchester.'

'Never been out of, or lived out of?'

'Been out of,' she said. 'Is that what you do – play cards? When you're not studying?'

'It's what I'm doing tonight. What about you – what do you do when you're not studying? Or are you like these guys and never leave the library?'

'I – I think your friend's arrived.'

'Bruno!' shouted Mike. 'Where the hell have you been?' He turned back to Katie. 'I'm going to have to go, but you're more than welcome to come along.'

'I don't think so,' she said, 'but thanks anyway.' She looked across to where Mike's mathematician friends were waiting. The new arrival – Bruno – was repeatedly jabbing at the upper arm of one of the others with his fist. 'Is he hurting that boy deliberately?' she asked.

'I think I'm needed,' said Mike. 'I'm going to have to go, but I'll see you around, okay?'

And Katie did see Mike around more often – in the library, in lectures – whether by chance or design, she didn't know. They didn't share any of the same seminars or tutorials – perhaps Katie just noticed him more? Mike was rarely alone, even in the library, and always seemed to have at least one or two hangers-on. Katie was curious – and also a little envious – to see how easy Mike was with other people. She began to see a pattern amongst Mike's friends; he was a magnet for students who would otherwise have found it hard to socialize in college. Katie recognized the type because she was one herself. Social misfits were comfortable in Mike's company. And not just from the Law Department. Eugene and Rory, Katie knew, were mathematicians, but she often caught sight of Mike outside the Medical Building, surrounded by students in white coats, and laughing, as ever.

Yet Mike never hit on Katie; there was just the occasional smile or a wave across campus. When they spoke again, it was Katie who approached Mike; she saw him alone, for once, surrounded by bound case histories in the library.

'So you do actually study law, then?' she asked.

'Tell me about it,' said Mike. 'Look at all this stuff! And getting your hands on it is impossible; people are ruthless when it comes to hiding these case files – just so they know where to find them for themselves.'

'It's worse than that,' said Katie. 'I think they're deliberately trying to sabotage any hope we might have of finding them.'

'Is that why you come and study in the middle of the night?'

'Partly,' said Katie, 'yes.' She smiled. 'How was the trip to the casino? Did you lose all your money?'

'It was disastrous,' said Mike. 'We never even got as far as hailing another cab. Bruno wouldn't leave them alone, and in the end I had to take Eugene and Rory home.'

'So you didn't get to hear Eugene's big secret?'

'No,' said Mike, 'but I didn't lose any money either. There'll be another time, I guess – so long as I can persuade Eugene to meet me again, that is.'

'And would you do that often – go gambling, I mean?'

'Well, not so often,' said Mike, 'but you have to do something, don't you? It can't all be work and no play. What about you – what do you do when you're not memorizing cases of English law?'

For the past three consecutive Saturdays Katie had gone on her own to the White Horse pub in Hulme.

There was something about the place that gave her the confidence to go in and, once inside, she felt so comfortable that she stayed. There were a few raised eyebrows – she was, after all, a white girl on her own in a black man's pub – but she was left alone. It was actually quite a mixed crowd and everybody was there for the music – a black dude of a DJ in a white suit and hat who played his favourite records on an old twin deck. Some people danced, but most just sat and listened and talked; it was a place where you could just be. It wasn't entirely a student-free zone, but it was good enough for Katie – she thought of the drinkers at the White Horse as real people. She drank vodka with orange and was happy; she gave off an air of self-containment and nobody bothered her.

She hesitated before letting Mike in on her secret, but went ahead anyway.

'If I ask you to meet me . . .' she began.

'I'd love to meet you,' said Mike.

'I can't . . . do anything,' said Katie.

'You wouldn't have to do anything,' said Mike. 'It'll be nice just to meet you away from the library for once.'

Katie smiled. She knew this was what she wanted, but it didn't come easily. But then she thought, well, she had to start somewhere – it might as well be with Mike.

'What are you doing with all those people?' she asked.

'All what people?' asked Mike.

'All the people you hang around with. Am I going to be an addition to your collection of freaks? Am I a weirdo too?'

'No, you're not a weirdo,' said Mike, 'and neither are they. They're all remarkable people, that's all.'

'Including that Bruno?'

'Bruno's . . . different, but still remarkable in some ways. He's troubled, I would say, rather than remarkable.'

'And me?' asked Katie. 'Am I remarkable?'

'Yes, I think so,' said Mike. 'I don't know why yet, but I think it's remarkable for some reason that you're here.'

'And you – how are you remarkable?'

'I'm remarkable in that I recognize remarkable people; it's very easy to miss them, you know.'

They agreed to meet the following Saturday.

But when it came to Saturday, Katie had a crisis and cut herself so much that she couldn't stop the bleeding. She hadn't been able to study all day and in the end had given up and gone to the gym, but however hard she pushed herself, she couldn't get meeting Mike out her mind. She told herself it was no big deal; there was no pressure and that Mike was safe – he wouldn't try anything. But telling herself was one thing, believing it was another. If she'd had a way of contacting Mike she would have cancelled, but she had no idea where he lived and hoping to see him around the campus was hopeless.

So at about eight o'clock she started getting ready and that was when the trouble began. Part of the problem was familiar to her – she was sick of her punk gear or, rather, she was sick of how the designers and copycats had hijacked what she liked to wear. Her clothes had once meant something to her, but now they were just a fashion statement. She went to see The Clash the previous year in the Apollo and she thought even they were a watered-down version of what she hoped they'd be – more or less inviting the audience to storm the stage during 'White Riot', manufacturing an event and packaging it for the press. Katie looked around her and saw all these other Katies falling for it – replica Katies from London who would be back in college tomorrow. And now here she was, doing exactly the same, dressing for rebellion while studying for a law degree. Part of Katie wanted this – to be just like everyone else – but what she really needed was to prove she was as good as everyone else if not better. She wanted to be normal, and yet somehow different.

'But you're not normal, are you?' Katie asked her reflection in the bathroom mirror. And she set about cutting herself again and again, until there was so much blood that she couldn't see the skin of her thighs and then she cried, with the pain but also the shame of being beaten, because she thought she could do this and now she knew she couldn't, so she rested her head on the bathroom shelf and let her arms drop between her legs and let the blade drop to the floor, and she stayed like that for a long time. And the worst wasn't over because she still had to clear up the mess, on her legs and on the floor, and because the moment had gone it was harder to face up to why she did this to herself, time after time, and she wished she could stop.

It was almost ten o'clock by the time Katie was clean and calm, and she still had to decide whether or not to go. What persuaded her in the end was her guess that Mike would be long gone – they were supposed to be meeting at nine – and also the knowledge that if she didn't go tonight, she'd have to do it all over again the next time. And there would be a next time; if she really wanted this there were things she had to go through. So she opted for the same plain look she'd worn for the day of registration, and no make-up; she looked pasty and washed out, but that couldn't be helped.

Mike was still waiting when Katie arrived. The bar was noisy and busy, but Katie saw Mike immediately, talking at the bar, and she walked over. She apologized for being so late.

'That's no problem,' he said. 'We're sat over there. What would you like to drink?' Mike saw the panic in Katie's face. 'Don't worry,' he said, 'it's only Eugene.'

Katie was relieved; the thought of a crowd scared her.

'How did you persuade Eugene to come?' she asked.

'Easy – I told him I was meeting you. He's smitten.'

'Don't be silly,' said Katie, but she blushed.

'Is that okay?' asked Mike. 'I thought you'd be more comfortable if it wasn't just the two of us, and Eugene's harmless; he's hardly said a word all night.'

Katie waited with Mike at the bar before joining Eugene at the table. When she said hello, Eugene murmured something and looked away, embarrassed. He picked up a pack of cards from the table in front of him.

Mike smiled.

'They're all scared of you at the bar,' he said to Katie. 'I asked them if you'd been in, and they knew who I meant straight away.'

'They're not scared of me,' said Katie.

'Well, wary then.'

'Because I'm a punk?'

'No, because you're . . . I don't know what you are. There's something about you that makes people – '

'Uneasy?'

'Wary, I said – edgy.'

'Which means uneasy. What about you – aren't you wary?'

'No,' said Mike. 'I don't do wary. This is a great pub – how did you find it?'

'Well, don't go telling everyone about it,' said Katie. 'The last thing I want is . . .' She didn't finish what she was about to say.

'What?' asked Mike. 'What's the last thing you want – a bunch of students moving in on your favourite pub?'

'I just like it here,' said Katie, 'that's all. I feel comfortable, even if I make them feel uneasy.' The idea that she intimidated the punters in the White Horse seemed silly to Katie. She hadn't yet learnt the effect she had on other people.

'You don't think much of students, do you?' asked Mike.

Katie shrugged.

'They're okay,' she said. 'I don't have that much to do with them, really.'

'You're studying for a four-year law degree,' said Mike. 'How can you not have much to do with them?'

'As little as possible, then,' said Katie.

'I'm a student,' said Mike, 'and so is Eugene.'

'Well, you're different.'

Katie didn't like students; she didn't like the idea of students. She thought of them as either spoilt rich kids supported by their parents, or freeloaders on a full grant. She resented anyone to whom anything came easy when things had been so hard for her. She saw kids – and they seemed like kids to Katie, though she was only a year or two older – intent on drinking their way through college and she couldn't understand them. She couldn't understand why they didn't appreciate just how lucky they were. She said as much to Mike.

'So you'll be happy when they do away with grants to students?' he asked. 'Because it's coming, you know, now that Thatcher's in power. We'll be given loans, not grants, to support ourselves.'

'We might appreciate it more,' said Katie.

'Yes,' said Mike, 'but what about the people who can't afford to take out a loan – what about them?'

'If they want it bad enough, they'll find a way.'

'Like you?'

'Yes,' said Katie, 'like me. Is there anything wrong with that?'

'Only how self-righteous you sound,' said Mike.

'What do you mean?'

'You received a grant, and had your fees paid.'

'But I'd have been a fool not to take it,' said Katie.

'And you think you'd still have gone to college, even if you had to pay the full course fees?'

'If that was what I wanted to do,' said Katie, 'then yes.'

'And what about someone without your ability?' asked Mike. 'Someone who doesn't have your self-sufficient, hard-as-nails ability to cope with whatever life might throw at them?'

'Come off it,' said Katie. 'We're not talking about people like that. We're talking about kids who are given everything and don't appreciate it – waste it even.'

'And you hate that, don't you?'

'Yes, I do, and I don't see anything wrong in hating it.'

'Why not just be happy for them?'

'Happy for them?'

'Yes, what's it to you?' asked Mike. 'So what if some kid's parents are loaded, and he squanders his allowance? So what if some other kid is given a full grant, and he chooses to drink it away? So what? Good luck to them!'

'It's wrong,' said Katie.

'It's only wrong if you worry that other people might have more than you, that someone else might have it easier than you. Why care about them? You have what you want, and you're doing what you want to do. Why not just be happy and proud of what you've achieved, instead of spoiling it with your begrudgery?'

'Oh, spare me,' said Katie. 'And what's begrudgery – is it what it sounds like?'

'You're the very definition of begrudgery,' said Mike. 'What – because you had it tough, you think everyone else should have it tough?'

'More or less,' said Katie, 'yes.'

'Why not think – I had it tough, so I hope no one else ever has to? Wouldn't that be a lot nicer?'

'That's not the way the world works,' said Katie.

'Oh,' said Mike, 'I can see you're going to fit right in. I bet you just can't wait to be a part of Thatcher's bold new Britain, can you? Fuck's sake, Katie, loosen up a little. Everybody should have a full grant, everybody should have shitloads of money, and no one should find life hard. There's money for all sorts of shit, so why not pay for everyone to go through college – or for everyone who wants to go through college?'

'But there are so many wankers here,' said Katie.

Mike smiled.

'Now, that's a different matter,' he said, 'and I have to confess: I'm a little disappointed on that front myself. I had this idea that college would be full of cool characters, like something out a Jack Kerouac novel, but you're right – there are too many wankers out there.'

'I take it you include me in that category?' said Eugene.

'No, Eugene,' said Mike, 'you're a geek; there's a difference. If you were a wanker then I wouldn't have asked you to come along tonight. Now, explain this card-counting trick to me. How is it done?'

Eugene had sat quietly all evening, shuffling the pack of playing cards over and over.

'It's not a trick,' said Eugene. He spoke down at the table, unable to look Katie in the eye.

'How about another drink first?' she asked.

'It's not a trick,' repeated Eugene. 'If it was a trick then it would involve some sleight of hand. A trick would be if I asked you to pick a card, and I managed to see it as you placed it back in the pack – that would be a trick.'

'Okay,' said Mike. 'We're agreed it's not a trick. Now could you please explain it to me in terms I might understand?'

'Something is not a trick when there is some logic or a skill attached to it,' said Eugene.

'But sleight of hand is a skill,' said Mike.

'But it's a cheating skill. It's deceptive and misleading and therefore dishonest.'

'Jesus, Eugene,' said Mike. 'Just show us the fucking thing, can't you?'

Katie laughed.

'Let me get the drinks in first,' she said.

Katie went over to the bar and noticed for the first time how space was made for her to get served. She paid for the drinks, and Mike appeared behind her to give her a hand.

'I told you,' he said, once they were back at the table. 'They're all scared of you.'

She ignored Mike, and turned to Eugene.

'Now,' she said, 'are you going to tell us about this card-counting theory of yours, or not?'

'Oh, it's not my theory,' said Eugene.

'But tell us anyway.'

'It's essential that you first understand the concept of not cheating.' He looked down at the table and seemed to be waiting for some response before going on. Katie looked at Mike, who raised his eyebrows.

'Eugene,' he said, 'we have nothing but the highest regard for you and your theory – or whoever's theory it might be. You're a mathematical genius, I know – '

'There are some maths involved, but it's at a very low level.'

'Well, good,' said Mike, 'because maybe then I can follow it.'

'For example,' said Eugene, and he placed the deck of cards on the table. 'There are fifty-two cards in that deck. The chances of picking out a certain card are one in fifty-two. If this lady would like to – '

'Her name's Katie,' said Mike.

'If she'd like to think of a playing card and then pick a card off the top of the deck?'

Katie did so.

'Is that the card you thought of?' Eugene asked the table.

'No,' said Katie, and smiled at Mike.

'But you can appreciate how the odds have now improved? There's a better chance that the next card might be yours?'

'Yes,' said Katie.

'Is that it?' asked Mike.

'No, said Eugene. 'I was simply illustrating how the odds might change.' He looked up and spoke directly to Katie for the first time. 'Could you put the card back and then shuffle the deck?'

Eugene watched Katie shuffle the cards.

'Mike,' he said, 'perhaps you'd like to shuffle the cards too; I don't think you were too impressed with the lady's – with Katie's shuffling skills?'

Katie handed the deck to Mike, and Eugene watched.

'Now what?' asked Mike.

'I can't state for certain where Katie's card will be, but I think you'll find it is in the lower third of the deck.'

Mike laughed. 'It's a good job you're not doing tricks, Eugene,' he said, 'because as tricks go, that one stinks – you know what I mean?'

'That wasn't a trick. I used my skill to follow the card as you shuffled the deck.'

'Well, can't you be a little more specific?'

'I am improving,' said Eugene, 'but for now my best guess is perhaps the top half of the bottom third.'

Katie took the deck off Mike and looked for the original card. It was fourteen off the bottom.

'That's incredible,' she said.

'And you really followed that card?' asked Mike.

'It's a skill, not a trick,' said Eugene. He was back to looking down at the table. 'It was quite easy to follow the first shuffle, as the card only moved the once. When

Mike shuffled, he also cut the deck a few times. I think he was trying to catch me out.'

'How accurate are you?' asked Mike.

'I was confident about the card being in the bottom third, the rest was an educated guess.'

'Educated?'

'Yes, because I think I took into account all the relevant factors.'

'And you were counting the cards?'

'No,' said Eugene, 'I was simply observing and remembering. I wanted to show you what could be achieved through trained observation.'

'So what about counting the cards?' asked Mike. 'How could watching the shuffle be of any use in a casino?'

'It couldn't – not unless you were very accomplished. If they saw you concentrating on the cards to that extent, they'd ask you to leave.'

Mike waited for Eugene to continue, but Eugene said nothing.

'So?' asked Mike. 'Are you going to tell us about the card-counting trick – the card-counting thing?'

'It's possible to observe which cards are laid down in a game of cards,' said Eugene. 'It's easier than tracing the shuffle of a deck. In a casino, the cards that have been laid down once cannot be laid down again until the dealer reaches the end of the deck; this tells us which cards are still there to be dealt.'

'But they use up to six decks in the shoe at a time,' said Mike.

'The same principles apply,' said Eugene. 'I'm not saying it's easy, I'm just saying it can be done.'

'The shoe?' asked Katie.

'The box from which the dealer gives out the cards,' explained Mike. 'Once the cards are shuffled, the shoe dispenses a card at a time; it prevents any sleight of hand by the dealer.'

'But what advantage could you hope to gain?' asked Katie. She looked first to Eugene and then to Mike.

'There is a way,' said Mike. 'In blackjack – or pontoon, as you might know it – or twenty-one, the advantage is with the player if there's a run of high cards. The house will always pay out over a certain number, say seventeen, and the dealer will never choose to go higher, for fear of going bust. You're likely to be dealt a better hand if the cards in the deck are higher, while the dealer is more likely go bust. But, Eugene,' he said, 'you'd have to be concentrating like fuck to remember all the cards that are laid down, and to think about your own game at the same time.'

'It's not essential to remember each individual card,' said Eugene. 'Experienced card counters all have a system – generally a plus or a minus value for all the low cards that have been dealt.'

'So you keep track of a running score?' asked Mike.

'And your running score counts for more the further into the deck you go,' said Eugene.

'Again?' said Mike.

'Just as Katie's chances improved after picking up that first card. If lots of low cards have come out the deck, there are lots of high cards still there to be dealt. But because there are fewer cards left in the deck, the odds are even better that you'll be dealt a high card. And that the dealer will go bust if he takes a third card.'

This was all beyond Katie.

'You're still talking odds,' she said. 'It's still a game of chance.'

'Yes,' said Eugene, 'but you've used your intelligence to make an educated guess.'

'And you'd put your money on that?'

'I wouldn't,' said Eugene. He sneaked a glance at Katie. 'But I think Mike would.'

Apart from Katie's vodka and orange once a week in the White Horse, her only outlet from study was the gym. The facilities were basic, primitive even by the standards of the late seventies, and the whole gym experience was different back then. This was not a hip place for beautiful young bodies to hang out and show off their tans; the gym was the preserve of sportsmen hoping to regain their strength after injury, and just a few serious bodybuilders – the gym was not a glam place to be seen by your friends. Katie had come across weight machines while she was still in care; using them was encouraged as a way of calming unsettled minds. She liked the solitude and she liked to push herself hard against the machines. What it did for her head, she didn't know – she was in such a mess anyway it could do her no harm. The facilities in the college were free and close to where she lived; she often carried her gear with her so she could call in on the way home from the library. There was a pool there too, but this was obviously out of bounds for Katie.

A few weeks after meeting Mike and Eugene in the White Horse, Katie saw their friend Bruno at the gym. She recognized him immediately but tried to make out she didn't know who he was. Bruno came over anyway.

'You're Mike's friend, Katie,' he said, and stood by her machine. He wasn't built like the rest of the guys in the gym. He was tall but not hugely built, more hard and wiry like Katie.

Katie stopped what she was doing. She wasn't comfortable with Bruno watching her, and she could feel his eyes on her body.

'You're Bruno,' she said.

Katie waited for him to speak or move away, but he did neither. She didn't want her sessions at the gym to be spoilt by Bruno being there each time.

'Well, I'll see you around,' she said.

Katie had no choice but to start up again on the machine. Bruno watched for a while and then walked away.

When Katie next met Mike, she asked him about Bruno.

'Who is he? What does he do?'

'He does law, the same as us.'

'But he's never at any lectures,' said Katie, 'or in the library.'

'No,' said Mike, 'I don't think Bruno's quite cut out

for college life. I can't see him making it through the first year, somehow – the first term, come to that.'

'But why?' asked Katie. 'Why bother getting onto the course in the first place?'

'You'd have to ask him that,' said Mike.

'I saw him at the gym; he gives me the creeps.'

'Yes, he told me,' said Mike. 'He also said you were rude.'

'I don't like him,' said Katie.

Mike smiled.

'Who do you like, Katie? Here,' he said, 'I've bought you a present, so you have to at least pretend to like me.'

Mike handed her a ticket; it was for a Buzzcocks concert the following week. Katie was delighted.

'Mike, thanks – but let me pay you for the ticket. Will you be there?'

'If you paid me for the ticket,' said Mike, 'then it wouldn't be a present, would it? And yes, I am going, but I have to warn you – Bruno's going too, and there'll be a big crowd of us.'

'Oh, I don't care,' said Katie. 'I'll be there.'

In all there were twenty of them in a row together, the strangest collection of people Katie had ever seen, particularly for a Buzzcocks concert. Katie saw Eugene and Rory; they were sat with two other students – who could only have been mathematicians – looking expectantly at the empty stage. Katie wandered through to the bar, but Mike was nowhere to be seen. Bruno was the only person she recognized.

'Did Mike buy tickets for all these people?' she asked him.

'Mike doesn't buy anything,' said Bruno above the noise, 'least of all tickets.'

'So how does he – '

'He'll have persuaded somebody, somewhere, that it was a good idea to let him have twenty tickets. Though why he thinks it's a good idea to invite some of these characters to this, I wouldn't know.'

'Why does Mike like mathematicians?' asked Katie.

'It's not just mathematicians,' said Bruno. 'Any egghead will do. I think Mike wishes he was good enough to be one of them.'

'A mathematician – Mike?'

Bruno shrugged. 'He's good, but he's not that good and he knows it. Most of these guys here' – he nodded in the direction of the others at the bar – 'are all business types, accountancy or banking and suchlike. A few medics but they tend to be chemists who just happen to be studying medicine.'

'Now there's something I never understood,' said Katie. 'Chemistry, I mean. All those symbols and that stupid periodic table – I just don't get it.'

'But everything in the world has to do with chemistry,' said Bruno. 'The glass you're holding, the drink you're drinking, the floor you're standing on, the air you're breathing, the smoke in the bar – everything. Every single thing in the world is made up of chemicals.'

'I think I must have had a poor teacher,' said Katie.

71

'Whatever the lesson, he'd always go back to amino acids or something like that, as though we all knew what the fuck he was talking about.'

'But he's right – we wouldn't be alive or here at this gig without the amino acids in our body.'

'Now you're at it.' Katie laughed. 'I don't see any other lawyers here.'

'No,' said Bruno. 'Mike can't stand lawyers. I sometimes think that's why he's studying law himself – so he never has to deal with another lawyer.'

'But we get in?' said Katie.

'Oh yes, we're special.'

'Where is he, anyhow?'

'Nice Guy Mike? He couldn't make it. One of his medical friends had a bit of an accident today.'

'What happened?' asked Katie.

'This guy is studying dentistry,' said Bruno. 'He gave an anaesthetic without reading the patient's notes, so – no more patient.'

'You mean he died?'

Bruno shrugged again as if to say – shit happens.

'So what's Mike hoping to do?' asked Katie.

'Make him feel better about himself?' suggested Bruno. 'Or at least not feel quite so bad. I don't know. As I say – Nice Guy Mike.'

Bruno knocked back his drink.

'Come on,' he said. 'Joy Division are the support band – they're the reason I'm here.'

Bruno walked away from the bar. Katie had wanted to ask him why he never attended any lectures – how he ever hoped to survive the course – but she didn't get the opportunity. She followed Bruno into the concert hall.

Katie had heard of Joy Division but she didn't know what to expect. She knew they were from Manchester and presumed they had the gig on the strength of that. A few hundred people came through from the bar but most of the crowd didn't bother. Eugene and the mathematicians, though, they were on their feet already, and Katie looked from them down to the stage and saw they were mimicking the actions of the singer. The music was harsh and disturbing. Katie had never heard music like this before, and she'd never seen anyone act like that on stage before. Part of her wanted to laugh, but then she saw Bruno's reaction: he was totally immersed in the music, his eyes closed and his head jerking forward like he was kicking someone on the ground.

They sang a song called 'She's Lost Control', and Katie had to sit down – images of cutting her legs flashed through her mind.

I have to stop doing this, she thought. I have to find a way to stop.

When the band finished, the mathematicians were ecstatic.

'Are you okay?' Bruno asked Katie.

'Yes,' she said. 'I need a drink.'

'That boy needs some help,' said Bruno, referring to the singer. Somehow this was more damning coming from Bruno, as though he knew a thing or two about needing help.

The Buzzcocks were disappointing in comparison – no, the Buzzcocks were just plain terrible. They stopped a song halfway through and the singer said it was shit.

'I agree,' said Bruno. 'Come on, let's go.'

The mathematicians shouted down obscenities to the stage, and all twenty of them left together – or eighteen, because Mike and his dentist friend were missing.

Bruno shook his head.

'What a fucking circus,' he kept saying. 'What a fucking circus.'

They all went into the bar for a drink.

Katie's first Christmas as a college student was hard. She was used to being on her own and this had never been a problem to her, but she hadn't realized how much she'd come to rely on Mike and, to a lesser extent, on Bruno for company. She felt the difference in their ages for the first time; for all Mike's sophistication, he seemed suddenly very young again when he told Katie he'd be returning to his parents' house in Belfast for the holidays.

'You know,' said Mike, 'you're more than welcome to come over to Belfast.'

Katie couldn't imagine what that would be like – Christmas amongst Mike's large extended family – but she knew it wasn't for her. She was grateful for his offer, but didn't like to think that he'd picked up on her loneliness.

'Bruno will still be around,' Mike told her. Katie had

developed a parallel friendship with Bruno, but she still wasn't quite at her ease in his company. She tried to avoid seeing him when they weren't all together in a crowd.

'It's not an issue,' she said.

'I've bought you a Christmas present,' said Mike, before he left. He handed Katie an envelope. 'It's a membership card for the new gym and fitness centre in town – brand new facilities and everything. You'll love it.'

'I don't want this,' said Katie, and then she corrected herself. 'I mean, thank you, but I don't want you to be buying me presents.'

'Well,' said Mike, 'if truth be told, I didn't actually buy it, and it's not just for you – we all have one, so we can all use the gym together.'

'You're going to start using the gym?' said Katie, and smiled.

'I will this one – you should see it.'

'And how did you get the membership?' she asked.

'It's part of a sponsorship deal, but that's not important.'

'Sponsorship deal – sponsorship for what? Oh, forget it! Look, Mike, I appreciate the thought, even if there's nothing wrong with the gym I use in the college, and it's closer, but I don't want you to be giving me things; I don't want you to be doing all these things for me.'

'But I like to,' said Mike.

'But I can't . . . I can't do anything for you.'

75

'You don't need to do anything for me; I'm not looking for anything from you.'

But this wasn't true, and they both knew it.

'You know what I mean,' said Katie. 'I can't let myself get close to you – to anyone.'

'I know that,' said Mike, and then, 'I just like you, that's all.'

Again, they both knew this wasn't true.

'But nothing will ever happen, Mike. I won't ever change, not ever.'

'I'm not asking you to change; I'm just giving you a Christmas present and I'd be happier if you accepted it. It'll be fun, you'll see, when we all get back in the New Year, and we can all hang out there together.'

In his own way Mike was anticipating the rising social scene of the gym, but he was also doing what he'd repeatedly done over the past few months: using their group of friends to involve Katie in an activity in which she felt safe. This was his way of helping her and she knew it.

'Thank you,' she said. 'Thank you. And I hope you have a great time with your folks over Christmas.'

She needed the gym membership once she realized the college facilities closed down for the holiday, and Mike was right – it was beautiful. Her beloved library, too, let her down, and she switched back to working in the library in town. There were fewer reference works to consult, but she had a workspace in which to complete her essays on time. She took to using the new gym once the library closed for the day.

Coming back from town one evening, she cut across from Oxford Road and crossed the Parkway by the footbridge rather than walking around by the road. As soon as she stepped onto the bridge she knew something wasn't right. Everywhere was quieter for a start, with few if any students around. There was less reason to be crossing from the college over into Hulme and, because this wasn't Katie's normal route, she hadn't been walking with her usual confidence and assurance. At the far end of the bridge she could make out somebody waiting in the dark. She hesitated and as she did so she knew she was in trouble. She slowed and considered turning back, but when she looked behind her there was another person following her. It was a classic mistake, one she'd heard talked about many a time in college whenever she mentioned she lived in Hulme. She thought about what she had on her – very little apart from some loose change in her purse. But then it occurred to her that it might not be money they wanted.

She stopped dead in the middle of the bridge. Her would-be attackers walked slowly towards her. She looked over the barrier down to the road below; it was way too high, but she would jump before she let them near her. She felt in her pocket for her keys and they seemed a very poor defensive weapon against two grown men. Then she fingered the razor blade around her neck and snapped it off the chain. Somebody else stepped onto the bridge from the college side and Katie laughed with relief when she saw it was Bruno. He walked alongside the person following Katie and without warning stamped his shoe into the side of their knee. Katie heard the crack above the noise from the traffic below, and the person slumped to the floor in pain. Bruno checked to make sure they stayed down, and walked on to Katie.

'You okay?' he asked. He smiled when he saw the blade in between her fingers. 'Nice one,' he said. 'Shall we go?'

They walked on along the bridge towards Hulme. The other would-be attacker thought better of taking on Bruno, and ran away.

Katie was still shaking when they reached her flat in Bonsall Street. She didn't need Bruno to tell her she'd had a lucky escape.

'You have to be more careful,' was all he said to her.

'I know. I will – and thanks,' she said. It was only after closing her door behind him that she thought it strange that Bruno should have been there to help her.

After what happened on the bridge, she adjusted her schedule to keep to more daylight hours; she had little choice anyway if she wanted to use the library. But she needed this remove – a separate place from home in which to study – and she needed the gym. It was hardly socializing, but staying at home alone wasn't enough for her anymore.

She was relieved not to see Bruno again over the Christmas holiday period. She didn't know where he would be, only that he wouldn't or couldn't be going home to his parents. If he'd received the same gym membership off Mike – and Katie presumed he had – he chose not to use it, or at least not at the same time as Katie. She knew Bruno had problems, but she didn't know what those problems were. She guessed they weren't so different to each other. She'd watched as his use of drugs intensified throughout the first term, but she didn't know what demons drove him on. She had to look after herself first and she was barely capable of that; the thought of trying to help Bruno as well was hopeless and, besides, he scared her.

2

Katie knew how important it was to Mike that she and Bruno at least got on well together. What she hadn't reckoned on, but what soon became obvious after that first Christmas vacation, was that being close to Bruno might leave Mike feeling threatened. No matter how much Katie protested, Mike believed she had a connection to Bruno that he didn't share.

'Oh for God's sake,' she said to Mike one night.

Katie realized again just how young Mike was. He might have been notoriously secretive in everything he did, but when it came to his feelings for Katie he was hopelessly transparent. There was little she could do to help him – the very idea that Mike should be jealous of Bruno was ridiculous, especially after trying so hard for them all to be friends. If this was what it meant to be in a relationship, she wanted no part of it.

Katie thought Mike seemed a little lost, as though something he'd seen back in Belfast had shocked him. Katie didn't know if this was personal or political – or perhaps it was a little of both – but Mike was less sure of himself. For a few weeks into the new term he had the look of someone who was not quite so sure of what he was doing – of how he came to be studying law in Manchester, or falling for a girl he couldn't even begin to understand.

After these first few weeks they settled back into a routine – the library, the gym and, increasingly, the casino – even if that routine was fuelled by a higher intake of a wide variety of drugs. Bruno naturally came into his own here, but at the time his drug consumption seemed no more excessive than Katie's studying or Mike's gambling; in their different ways, they were each as freakishly singular as the other.

Mike was generous when it came to sharing the proceeds from whatever mad scheme might take his fancy.

'If only you put as much energy into your studies,' said Katie, but she knew how quickly Mike became bored. It was as though having got to college – even at so young an age – Mike was only interested in doing the minimum amount of work necessary. There was always some new idea, something somebody somewhere had told him, that Mike just had to get into.

Katie only ever picked up scraps of information as to what Mike might be up to. His explanation of the sponsorship deal for the gym in town, for example, nowhere near explained their membership of such an exclusive club.

'Who are they sponsoring?' asked Katie. 'Or who's sponsoring them – how does it work?'

'The gym are sponsoring the Law Department,' said Mike.

'To do what?'

'To do nothing – to be the Law Department.'

'But you can't make deals for the Law Department,' said Katie, 'and, besides, most of us aren't even studying law.' As Bruno had pointed out, most of Mike's friends were scientists of one form or another – mathematicians, chemists, medics – as well as a few accountants and business types.

'They don't need to know,' said Mike. 'I gave them a list of twenty names, and in return for that they get an association with a prestigious university department. It doesn't cost them anything and they can brag about it on their notepaper – or in their ads, things like that.'

'But who did you ask if this was okay?' asked Katie.

'No one,' said Mike. 'I just used some departmental headed paper.'

'But what if you're found out?'

'I won't be – how could we be? Plus,' Mike added, 'I didn't give them our real names.'

Katie had noticed the incorrect details on her membership card.

'But that's fraud,' she said. 'Worse – you've included all your friends in the fraud.'

Mike shrugged.

'I don't see anyone complaining,' he said. 'You can give me back your membership, if that's what you want, but it would be a shame.'

This was true – Katie loved their trips into town and it was so much more fun than the solitary exercise of her first term at college. It often got out of hand though, and more than once they'd been asked either to cool it or to leave. She couldn't imagine this was what the gym had hoped for in sponsoring the Law Department – certainly not when Bruno was around.

'But whoever heard of sponsoring a university department?' she asked.

'Oh,' said Mike, 'I think you'll see a lot more of that in the future. We got in first, that's all, and as I say – it's costing them nothing.'

'But what – '

'But, but, but,' said Mike. 'If we get found out, we get found out; until then we just enjoy it.'

On the rare occasions that Mike was open and frank with Katie, she was left with more questions than she was given answers. They continued to visit the White Horse on a Saturday night and it became their thing, the one time on their own together. They might go on to meet the others at a casino in town, but Katie liked the times she spent alone with Mike. She didn't feel under any pressure; she was comfortable with him, despite everybody knowing how close they'd become.

'Mike,' she asked one night, 'where do you get all your money from? Are your parents loaded?'

Mike laughed.

'You'll be glad to hear that I'm completely self-supporting – well, apart from having my fees paid for by the government.'

'So where does all your money come from?' Katie asked.

'Well I . . . I don't receive a maintenance grant as such,' said Mike, 'but I do get some money for being from Northern Ireland at a college in Britain. And because I'm Irish – because I have Irish citizenship – I get some money for that too.'

'You have Irish citizenship?'

'Yes,' said Mike, 'and British.'

'How can you have both?' asked Katie.

'It's worse than that,' said Mike. 'I'm also a US citizen because I was born in the States.'

'You don't get money from them too, do you?'

'No, not directly,' said Mike, 'but I do have a scholarship with an American company with an office in Belfast.'

'A law company?'

'No, a stockbroker – or an investment banker as they like to call themselves.'

'And they're paying for you to get through college?' asked Katie.

'They're paying something towards it,' said Mike, 'and I've agreed to go work for them when I graduate.'

'In Belfast?'

'Or London, or the States – they decide.'

'But what does a stockbroking firm want with a law graduate?'

'Everybody needs a lawyer, Katie; you should know that.'

'And is that what you want to do – work for an American stockbroking firm?'

'Not forever,' said Mike, 'but it's as good a place as any to start.'

'That's hardly what I call self-supporting,' said Katie.

'Well, it is in that I've used my initiative to make life easier for myself.'

'Oh, you're good at that,' said Katie. 'It still doesn't explain how you have enough money to go gambling several nights a week.'

'I don't gamble,' said Mike. 'I play to win.'

'You do gamble,' said Katie. 'I've seen you. It's not only blackjack you play; I've watched you place a whole night's winnings on the roulette table.'

'That's just for a bit of fun. You have to take a risk every now and again.'

'Whatever,' said Katie. 'You still seem to have a lot of money – more than you should have.'

'You only have to look for it,' said Mike.

'What does that mean?'

'It means that there's money to be had, if only you're prepared to take it.'

'I still don't understand,' said Katie. 'Where are they giving money away?'

'The banks, for one,' said Mike. 'They were only too keen for me to open an account when I started college, so I opened several.'

'Under your own name?'

'Some, but not all.'

'How many accounts did you open?'

'Quite a few,' said Mike. 'About thirty, I think.'

'Thirty?' said Katie. 'But what's the point – you can only take out what money you put in, surely?'

'Not necessarily – the banks are so slow in clearing funds, half the time they don't know what you might have in the bank. I create such a convoluted trail of accounts, I can disappear with their money before they figure out what's happening.'

'But it all leads back to you, doesn't it?' asked Katie.

'No,' said Mike. 'I keep my own accounts completely separate. Most of the others are bogus business accounts.'

'Now that is fraud,' said Katie. 'They can put you in jail for that, or throw you out of college – Mike!'

'Don't worry,' he said. 'I won't be going anywhere near those accounts again.'

'So what now?' asked Katie. 'What mad, illegal scheme are you dreaming up now?'

'Not illegal,' said Mike. 'I earn a fair bit at the casino, but nothing too spectacular; and I have a broker buying and selling shares on my behalf. Together, they make a lot of money; certainly more than I need to support myself through college.'

'A broker?' asked Katie.

'Yes.'

'From your Belfast firm?'

'No,' said Mike. 'I don't want them to know about it. I have someone based in London.'

'And he advises you on what to buy and sell?'

'Occasionally, but it's mostly my own decisions.'

'So what – you study the *Financial Times* each day, or something?'

'Yes,' said Mike, 'I do, but a lot of it is just common sense.'

'Mike!' said Katie.

'What?'

'There's nothing common sense about it! You're studying for a law degree, for Christ's sake.'

'So? I'm doing okay on the course; maybe not up to your standards, but I'll pass the end-of-year exams.'

'But what if you get caught?'

'Caught at what?' asked Mike. 'I told you, I've stopped with the banks thing, though they're so stupid it's tempting to rip them off all over again.'

'Promise me you won't,' said Katie.

'Why?'

'Because I don't want you to lose everything, and I don't want to lose you.'

Mike looked up at Katie.

'I mean,' she said quickly, 'I don't want you to be kicked off the course.'

Mike took a moment to reply.

'They won't kick me off the course,' he said. 'I'm not going anywhere. Unlike Bruno – I think he's had his final warning.'

'Really? Do you think so?' asked Katie. 'Won't they wait until after the exams? At least give him until the end of the year?'

Mike shook his head.

'No,' he said. 'From what I heard this morning, I think Bruno's gone.'

Bruno was gone, in more than one sense of the word. Katie couldn't understand how he had ever hoped to hold down his place on the course; couldn't see why he had even applied to study law in the first place. He was obviously very intelligent, but was in a permanent state of self-destruct. Katie felt uneasy in his company, particularly when they were alone. He'd never actually done anything to upset her, but she could sense the potential for him to do so. Part of it was sex: Bruno fancied Katie and showed it. Everyone else – Eugene, for example – was either embarrassed by Katie's good looks, or presumed she was with Mike and therefore off-limits.

Katie recognized that Bruno's self-harm was much more public than her own; she didn't know if it was any the worse for that, or any better.

Katie never understood why Mike gave Bruno so much of his time. Mike was under no obligation to explain his every action to Katie, but it was unlike him to do anything that wasn't in his own interest. If the crowd of them were out together – at the casino, say – it was obvious to Katie that Bruno acted as a form of protection; otherwise, they were just a bunch of nerds let loose on the town. But Bruno was also such a wind-up merchant that he could never resist having a dig at the likes of Eugene and Rory. Bruno wasn't always happy to be seen out with them, and they would certainly have been happier without him.

But Bruno was also there for Mike's own personal protection. Mike was always just one step away from being in a scrape with some dealer in the casino and Bruno's presence was an unnerving deterrent to anyone starting trouble. The pit bosses – the floor managers

– weren't quite so in awe. It was their job to watch out for the likes of Mike and forcibly eject them from the casino. All Bruno could do then was provide a barrier while Mike got out with his winnings; it could get pretty intimidating when they asked you to please accompany them to some back room. It got really ugly once after they'd repeatedly been playing a Chinese casino in town – Bruno was no match for twenty or so baseball bats and they all ran out as fast as they could, winnings or no winnings. Bruno often caused more trouble than he prevented; he was forever being guided out of a club or a casino, with Mike pleading for him to please just walk away.

If Katie thought they would be seeing less of Bruno once he was thrown off the course, she was wrong. Nothing much seemed to change. Katie suspected that Mike felt sorry for Bruno – as she suspected he had her when they first met – and that this was what bound the three of them together. Was this the basis of Mike's friendship with Bruno and Katie – a sympathy bordering on pity? Mike denied it, but the impression remained.

At the end of the first year Mike persuaded Katie to hold a party in her flat and, despite reservations about her privacy, she agreed.

'It'll be fine,' said Mike. 'Everybody will be so drunk or high, they won't be looking in your drawers and things.'

'Great,' said Katie, 'so they'll be throwing up in my bathroom?'

'If they make it that far,' said Mike, and smiled. 'I promise you we'll all help tidy up, and who else has a place like yours? It's ideal for a party.'

Katie felt as protective of her flat as she did of the White Horse – this was her space and she wanted it to remain so. But she understood what Mike was doing. He was right: Katie's flat was the ideal place for a going-away party, but this had more to do with Katie loosening up and not being so uptight amongst their friends. She'd never looked at her things through the eyes of other people before; even Mike was a rare enough visitor to her flat, and only once got past the front door.

'I need to use your loo,' he said, after he'd walked Katie home one night.

'Well, you can't,' she said.

'What do you mean, I can't? I have to.'

Katie stood in the doorway and looked at Mike. Their friendship demanded that she let him in. She was scared that he might see something he shouldn't, some incriminating evidence she may have left lying around in the bathroom. It was decision time again: let Mike in, or retreat back into her own private world. She stepped back and allowed him through.

'I didn't snoop around,' Mike said when he came back down. 'I just concentrated on my aim.'

The party raised the same issues for Katie, only on a larger scale; but at least she had time to prepare for it.

'It'll be fine,' repeated Mike. 'You'll be fine. Everybody hides their stuff before a party. Clear away as many things as you can and by the time we arrive in from the pub, we won't notice a thing.' He seemed to be saying that it was normal for Katie to have her secrets, that he understood her need for privacy and it was fine – but then he didn't know her secrets, did he?

'You're not all meeting in the White Horse?' she asked.

'Where else would we go?' said Mike. 'Come on, Katie, I'll talk to the bar staff; they won't mind a crowd of students in for one night.'

'No,' said Katie, 'but I might.'

'But these are our friends,' said Mike.

Katie thought of what Mike had said as she got the flat and herself ready for the party. It helped her avoid repeating the disaster of their first night out together. It was normal to strip the flat bare of anything that could be damaged; it was normal to hide any personal stuff she didn't want to be seen – this is what people did when they held a party in their home. But it was inside her head that Katie feared the most; there was nothing normal about what went on there.

Why did Mike push it so? Why did he keep putting her in a position where she had to confront what she did to herself? She thought she knew, but she didn't understand – how could anyone in his right mind fall for her? He couldn't possibly know – could he?

When the moment came – that look in the mirror before she dressed – Katie tried to slow it down. She wanted to freeze that precise moment – now, is it now? She wanted to know the exact second. She wanted to know what made her reach for the bathroom cabinet. Was it fear of what the evening might bring? She thought of the girls in *The Great Gatsby* – girls who knew that an evening would soon be over, that a party would always end, that none of it really mattered at all.

Katie thought of Mike. She didn't want him to know what she did to herself; she didn't want him to see the cuts on her thighs. Well, it was too late for that; her scars would never heal.

It's not as though he'll ever see you naked, she thought. Not tonight – and not ever?

Katie didn't want to keep doing this to herself. She didn't want to live her life in this way. She wanted to use her intelligence to beat this thing.

She looked in the mirror, but her reflection laughed at her.

In the end it was the thought of the bloody mess that slowed the moment down.

If you do this now, she thought, if you lose it now, then you have to clean up the blood. You have to wash yourself and clean the floor; you have to check for splashes, and you'll be crying so you won't be able to see.

It would add an hour on to getting ready, and Katie would be late for the pub; there was every chance that people might start arriving at her flat.

Katie looked down at her thighs.

Don't look down there! You know what's down there – nothing's changed there. Are you going to do this, or what? Is this the moment?

Katie reached for the door to the bathroom cabinet. She looked hard at her reflection in the mirror and felt for the packet of razor blades. She unwrapped the blade and held it between her thumb and forefinger. She lowered her arm so that her hand lay flat against her right thigh. She pressed the cold metal surface of the blade against her skin.

'This is the moment,' she said, and she moved the edge of the blade across her skin. The blood trickled over her fingers. This was too good a feeling for Katie ever to stop; this was her sex. It hurt, but she hadn't lost control.

When Katie arrived at the White Horse, she was relieved to see that Bruno wasn't there. The last thing she wanted was Bruno starting trouble, completely off his head on some drug or other. Not that Katie was a saint when it came to drugs, and Bruno kept her supplied with whatever she might need, but Bruno took everything to excess. Katie couldn't keep track of what he was on, and he could turn a harmless occasion into an unpleasant scene within seconds of arriving.

This had happened a few weeks before the party, when Katie was at the gym in town. Bruno turned up, and Katie saw immediately what a volatile state he was in. He was always worse when Mike wasn't around; or rather, he was always in the same state, and only Mike had the ability to talk him around. Bruno began by muttering something to the rhythm of his weight machine; each time he brought his arms together, he repeated this one phrase. At first, the noise of the gym obscured what Bruno was saying, but he grew louder and louder with each rep. Katie hoped the exercise would act as a distraction for Bruno, but she could see he was getting worse.

'I wanna fucka nigga,' he said. 'I wanna fucka nigga.'

Katie heard what it was that Bruno was chanting. She stopped her tread machine and grabbed her towel. Bruno's chant became a shout, and Katie ran into the changing room. She sat and listened to the disturbance outside in the gym – Bruno's shouts of protest, and the scuffle as the other members threw him out. They didn't even wait to call security.

Why would Bruno do such a thing? Or say such a thing? Katie found out later the same day that Bruno had been thrown off the course, but this didn't even begin to justify or excuse his behaviour. She knew that somehow she was mixed up with all the things in Bruno's head, but if Bruno was sweet on Katie, he had a strange way of showing it. Unlike Mike, Katie felt no pity for Bruno at times like this – only disgust.

Katie knew that Bruno would appear at some point on the night of the party; she just didn't want it to be at the White Horse.

'He feels really bad about that day at the gym,' said Mike.

'And so he should,' said Katie. 'I just don't see how you – '

'Yes, yes, I know,' said Mike. 'You don't know why I

bother with Bruno. But he thinks the world of you, you know.'

'And he thinks a stunt like that will make me like him more?'

'He's trying to get your attention,' said Mike. 'He wants you to at least notice him once in a while.'

'Is he stupid?' asked Katie.

'No,' said Mike, 'he's not stupid, but he loses the run of himself when you're around. He doesn't know how to cope with you – just as you don't know how to cope with him.'

Katie knew that sooner or later she had to come clean with Bruno, and let him know that nothing was ever going to happen between them. She knew he wouldn't be as understanding as Mike; Bruno could never have a relationship with a woman without sex.

But later, when he arrived at the party, Bruno was quiet and almost respectful of being in Katie's home. When he took the time to talk to Katie properly – as he had at the Buzzcocks concert – she found him to be good company and a breath of fresh air. At times like this Katie liked having Bruno around; he lent an edge to their group, and suddenly the party was alive and full of potential.

'I'm so sorry about the gym,' he said to Katie. 'It was a stupid thing to do, and I apologize.'

'It's nothing to do with me,' said Katie. 'It's the other members you should be apologizing to.'

'I know, I know,' said Bruno, 'and I have. I've spoken to everybody who was there, and I've written to the gym to apologize. They say they're reviewing my membership.'

'But why would you do such a thing?' asked Katie.

Bruno shook his head.

'I don't know. Sometimes I just . . . lose it.'

Well, Katie could understand that.

'But what a thing to say,' she said.

'I know,' said Bruno. 'It was unforgivable – and I'm sorry.'

But, by the end of the party, Bruno had reverted to type. As people left, the farewells were full of drunken assurances to meet up again through the summer. Katie played along, though she knew it was just so much bullshit. She was too tired for goodbyes. Mike was asleep on the sofa, and Katie wished he'd wake up; he'd pick up on her mood and know how to get rid of the few remaining guests. Everybody was going back to the security of their parents' houses and summer jobs and, perhaps, holiday trips abroad. Mike was returning to Belfast as part of his agreement to work for the firm sponsoring him through college; only Katie and Bruno were staying in Manchester, just as they had at Christmas.

Bruno walked through to the kitchen and grabbed a six-pack of beer from the fridge. Katie was in the hallway, saying goodbye to Eugene, and Bruno pushed past to leave.

'Oh right,' said Katie. 'Just take the last of the beer, why don't you?'

Bruno turned at the door.

'What are you saying?' he asked.

'It's not like you brought anything with you in the first place,' said Katie.

Bruno dropped the cans to the floor. He grabbed Katie by the neck, and pinned her to the wall of the hallway. Katie's feet were lifted from the ground, and she struggled to take her weight on her toes. She couldn't breathe because of Bruno's grip on her throat. He had his other arm drawn back to hit her.

'You sh-shouldn't,' said Eugene, and tried to block Bruno's fist.

'Fuck off, Eugene!' said Bruno.

'Bruno!' shouted Mike. He ran through from the other room.

Bruno stared at Katie.

'Let her go,' said Mike. 'Put her down.'

Bruno shifted his grip so he held Katie up by her jaw. She could breathe, but she was still unable to reach the floor with her toes. She spoke to Bruno through her clenched teeth.

'Go on, then,' she said. 'Fucking do it, why don't you? Get it over with, you cunt!'

'I fucking will, you bitch!' said Bruno.

'Bruno!' shouted Mike.

Bruno lowered his arm and relaxed his grip on Katie. She slumped against the wall.

'Give me a cigarette,' he said to Eugene.

'I – I don't have one,' said Eugene. 'I don't smoke.'

'Here,' said Mike and offered a packet to Bruno. 'Now calm down, for Christ's sake.'

Bruno took a cigarette, lit it, and drew heavily on it. He stared down at Katie and she stared back. Everybody stayed as they were, and waited for Bruno to decide what to do. He took three long drags on the cigarette, and threw the butt out the open front door.

'Thanks for the party,' he said, and leant down to pick up the cans of beer.

'Leave the beer,' said Katie.

Bruno shook his head. 'If Mike wasn't here, you'd be dead,' he said to Katie.

'I know,' said Katie. 'You're a hard man; we all know. But I still want my beer.'

Bruno shrugged and laughed, and then walked out the door.

'Katie!' shouted Mike. 'Let him go – it's not worth it.'

Katie sensed Eugene trembling next to her by the door, and she turned her attention to him.

'It's okay,' she said to him, 'it's okay.' She led Eugene back into the flat and sat him down. The others in the room mumbled their farewells to Katie and Mike. The party was over now, that was for sure.

'Would you like me to stay?' asked Mike.

'No, I'd like you to make sure Eugene gets home okay.'

'I want to stay,' said Mike. 'I could take Eugene home and then come back. I could help you clear up.'

Katie shook her head. They both knew what he was talking about.

'I don't want you to,' she said. 'I want to be on my own.'

When they'd left, she stood in the hallway where Bruno had pinned her to the wall. She'd been scared, but she'd felt something else too and she finally understood her relationship with Bruno. For a brief moment she had wanted him to touch her. If he'd lowered his arm and touched her, with his fingers and not his fist, or maybe even his lips, she wouldn't have stopped him – even with Mike there, so close by. She reached up now to her own lips and smiled.

Well now, there's a thing, she thought.

But nobody would ever know, and she'd never let herself be caught out like that again.

The summer gave them all a chance to cool off. Mike arranged for Katie to work for his American company, or a subsidiary of it, in Manchester.

'Why would I want to work for an investment banker?' she asked.

'Why not – what else are you going to do?' said Mike. 'I doubt there's a case of English law you haven't read and memorized and, anyway, don't you need the money?'

This last was a consideration – Katie was tired of just existing. Three months was a long time to wait before her next grant cheque, and signing on for the dole seemed like a step back into dependency, back into care.

'But why would they want me?' she asked.

'Because I told them how suitable you are,' said Mike.

'On what grounds? I don't even know what they do.'

'On the grounds that every workplace is the same.'

'And what would you know about that?' asked Katie. 'You're only just out of nappies.'

Mike smiled.

'Ouch,' he said. 'Point taken – that last bit I picked up from my father.'

'And what does he do?' asked Katie.

'He's a management consultant, so he knows about these things. He reckons that once you start a job, you find out just how easy it is and how useful you really are.'

'Have you ever had a job, Mike?'

'Yes,' he said, 'I have, but this isn't about me. Who knows, you may even like it.'

This was Mike, forcing the issue again; he wouldn't allow Katie the easy option of staying hidden away at home.

'Katie,' he said, 'you're studying for a law degree. If you do nothing else with your life, that's already more than most people ever hope to achieve. But what will you do next? I know it's several years away, but what's going to happen once you graduate? You're not going to sit in a flat in Hulme, staring at a graduation certificate pinned to your wall – or are you? I don't know – perhaps you want to become some big, flash, corporate lawyer, or maybe help disadvantaged children. I don't know, and it doesn't really matter. But you're going to have to learn to live out there in the world, and this is as good a way as any. Otherwise, what's the point in trying in the first place?'

Katie smiled.

'Fine speech, Mike,' she said.

'Well . . .'

Katie knew he was right and she was glad that he cared, but in the end it was the money that made up her mind – that and the fact there were now over two million people on the dole. She was lucky to be given the option of working, and she found that she liked it. She learnt a lot and was a natural, it seemed, when it came to the principles of banking. The company offered to sponsor Katie for the next three years in college. She told Mike when they met up again after the summer.

'It's in their own interest,' said Mike. 'They wouldn't do it unless they saw something in it for them.'

Katie had enjoyed working, but it was good to be back in college, back to her studies, and good to see her friends again. Even Bruno was still around, though for now he kept his distance from Katie. She knew he attended the gym regularly, because she saw his false name signed in at reception, but she never saw him there again. She next saw him a few weeks into the new term and she was surprised, because it was on campus.

'Did Bruno apply to do another course?' she asked Mike.

'No, he's working for me now.'

'Working for you – doing what?'

'I'm starting a listings magazine for Manchester,' said Mike.

'A what?' asked Katie.

'A listings magazine – like *Time Out* in London.'

'But that's London,' said Katie. 'Is there enough happening in Manchester to justify a full magazine?'

'Well, we're going to have articles and stuff, but yes, Manchester has enough going on – more than enough over the next few years. I got the idea from that concert we went to – or you all went to. If Manchester's producing the best bands in the country then people will want to see them; they won't want to miss out on what's happening.'

'But that singer's dead,' said Katie. 'He hanged himself.'

'That was unfortunate,' said Mike, 'but there are others on the way. And there are new clubs opening; things are happening, believe me.'

'Yes,' said Katie, 'but we never go – it's just for the tourists. And when we do go there are only about twenty people there. It's hardly what you'd call a movement.'

'You might not go,' said Mike, 'but I do, and I tell you, something is definitely happening here. You're just pissed off because punk is dead, and you can't cope with the fact that something new might be happening without you. Why do you think all these Londoners want to come to college in Manchester?'

'Okay, okay, I get the point,' said Katie, 'but how do you go about setting up a magazine? And what do you mean – Bruno's working for you?'

'I'm responsible for raising the finance, persuading investors that it's worth their while.'

'And what does Bruno do – stand beside you to help persuade them?'

'No,' said Mike. 'Bruno's doing two things: he's making sure the venues notify us with details of what's on, and he's working with the writers on their articles for the first edition.'

'The writers?' asked Katie.

'Mostly people in college studying journalism or suchlike.'

'You mean those wasters that you see in the coffee bar all day?'

'Yes, those wasters. You know, Katie, sometimes you're not very nice. Just because someone doesn't fit your profile of the conscientious student doesn't mean they have nothing to offer.'

'It sounds like a charity project for Bruno.'

'As I said – that's not very nice. I wouldn't be doing this if I didn't think it could make me a lot of money.'

'How – how can it make you money?'

'Selling advertising space, selling the whole magazine if it takes off – though naturally I haven't told that to anybody else.'

Mike was a strange mixture – since coming back to college Katie had noticed how much more politicized he'd become. He was as exercised by the striking steelworkers as he was by events in the North. Yet self-interest was never far away; accumulating money, legally or otherwise, was what drove him on. The idea for the magazine probably originated as a way to help out Bruno, but Mike couldn't be involved in something for long without thinking how it could make money. So while he may not have liked the direction society was heading, he was ideally placed to benefit from it.

The magazine was a success, but suffered from a lack of investment. Mike wanted it to work well enough to attract a major buyer; it was a good idea, but it became a drain on his resources. Bruno had done well, but he was bored already and likely to go off the rails at any given time. His drugs intake was phenomenal and it was impossible for him to sustain a regular lifestyle.

Their trips to casinos continued, but they were becoming less welcome wherever they went. This was partly due to their behaviour — there was always someone who had drunk too much or taken too many drugs — but the pit bosses also recognized Mike as a consistently big winner, and they didn't like it. Katie saw that the purpose of their large group was to distract attention away from Mike as the main player, but twice now Mike had been told that they didn't want to see him again. He was doing nothing illegal, and they weren't exactly sure how he was managing it, but it was up to the casinos if they wanted him on their premises.

Mike bankrolled the casino visits but it was on the understanding that if you went along, you had to work for your supper. Based on what Eugene had told Mike in the White Horse, they all sat at various blackjack tables and kept count of the cards passing through the shoe. If a low card was played, that added to the positive count; if a high card was played, that took away from the count. Anything more sophisticated would have been apparent to the casino and impossible for the players to keep track of, but it did tell them if there were mostly high cards left in the shoe. Mike stepped into the game when he was given a signal that the cards were in his favour.

As it was, some of Mike's friends were of more use to him than others – the likes of Eugene saw it as a fascinating mental challenge, while Rory would get carried away with the game and forget to keep count. There were advantages in even this. It was sometimes obvious to the pit bosses that Eugene was keeping track of the cards, but he won so little, it was of no consequence. In fact, more often than not, Eugene lost; but he lost only small amounts of money, while Mike never played with less than a hundred on each bet. And if the others couldn't give Mike such good information, they at least acted as a distraction and confused the casino into thinking they weren't with Mike. Best of all, though, were Katie and Bruno; they were accurate counters without appearing to be so. Katie looked stunning and Bruno looked dangerous – it took longer for the casino to pick up on Mike when these two were around.

But there were frustratingly small returns for Mike. It was possible to view each trip to the casino as a bit of fun where he made a little money, but still he wanted more. Mike had Eugene make out probability tables he could memorize, colour-coded charts that Mike studied more closely than the *Financial Times*. He often played with several hands when the shoe was in his favour, but the possibility of really taking the casinos for a serious amount of money was still tantalizingly out of his reach.

'There are too many variables remaining,' said Eugene. 'You require a more accurate count.'

'Yes,' said Katie, 'but unfortunately we're not operating under laboratory conditions.'

Mike tended to agree – anything more sophisticated would be too easy for the casino to spot, and more likely to lead to mistakes.

'The problem is,' said Mike, 'I need a large enough bankroll to see me through the bad patches. Even when the count is good, I still sometimes lose.'

'You could flip a coin forever,' said Eugene, 'and you would bet on it landing on heads at least once, but it might only ever land on tails.' He spoke as if in awe of this statistical possibility.

'Or,' said Mike, 'and this is more likely, it could land on tails until I ran out of money, and then land on heads,' said Mike. 'I don't know; I think I make more money on the stock market than I do in the casino.'

Katie thought of pointing out that this was maybe the way it should be, but she knew Mike could never let it go; he was convinced of some golden payday in the future. They started travelling further afield, first to Leeds and then to London, where at least they weren't so well known. Mike couldn't cover the cost for them all to go on these trips, so he took Bruno and Katie, who were more use to him; for Katie, the trips held the added attraction of seeing other cities for the first time.

Katie eventually made her peace with Bruno – she had to if she was to spend time with Mike. By the end of their second year, the group had crystallized into a friendship between these three. Katie was never totally at her ease in Bruno's company, and avoided being alone with him for any length of time, but she knew she was not the easiest of characters herself. Whatever chemistry had brought them all together in the first place – and Katie continued to believe that chemistry was Mike – the dynamic held strong for the three of them.

Bruno continued to stretch Katie's tolerance to the limit. He turned up at a drinks party to celebrate the end of that year's exams, and deliberately antagonized Rory with Irish jokes. It was the time of the hunger strikes, and Bruno's jokes split the room in two; some laughed, while the others felt as though they shouldn't.

'What's Bobby Sands' phone number?' Bruno asked.

Rory looked away and didn't answer.

'Ate nothing, ate nothing, ate nothing,' said Bruno.

Rory wasn't strong enough to stand up to Bruno, and besides Bruno was too high to care. Katie watched and listened from across the room. Bruno saw her looking and smiled, but Katie didn't smile back.

'What?' asked Bruno, but Katie said nothing.

She already knew that, come the following year, Rory and Eugene were likely to drift away – not so much because of Bruno but the ever-increasing demands of college work. Katie only saw them occasionally around the campus, or less often at the gym; for the most part Rory and Eugene's wild days were over.

Mike cited the hunger strikes as his reason for choosing to work in Manchester that summer, but Katie thought there was more to it than that. She suspected Mike had a sweetheart back home in Belfast, though if he did, he wasn't saying. Katie and Mike worked together as traders in the stockbroking firm, but Mike's heart wasn't in it. Katie, on the other hand, became the star trainee in the company, and it was obvious she had a future there if she wanted it.

Mike taught Katie how to drive – another example of her new found confidence – and she passed her test at the first attempt. Mike bought an old Jaguar for next to nothing – not for him any old student runaround. It cost Mike more in petrol than it had to buy. They often drove out to the hills after work, and called into village pubs for some supper – they appeared to be quite the couple. Katie loved spending time with Mike, especially working together throughout the summer, but she was worried about where he hoped it was all heading. She suspected he'd stayed in Manchester out of misplaced jealousy of Bruno, which was crazy, but just as crazy was Katie allowing this to continue.

It was a strange time. Katie and Mike avoided the

celebrations on the day of Charles and Diana's wedding. They escaped in the Jag, up into the hills, as far away as possible from the madness of the street parties. It was hard to believe that in another part of the United Kingdom men were deliberately starving themselves to death for the right to wear their own clothes in prison.

Towards the end of that day Katie and Mike sat in the car, high in the Pennines above Manchester, and looked out over a reservoir. Katie was in the driver's seat, Mike in the passenger's.

'Mike?' asked Katie. 'Why do you spend all your free time with me?'

Mike didn't reply.

'What's the point,' she asked, 'when there's nothing in it for you?'

Mike looked away, down to where the evening sun was reflected in the water of the reservoir.

'Because,' said Katie, 'if you're hoping that some day there might be, then I have to tell you – there won't.'

'I know,' said Mike. 'You've made that clear enough, often enough. I know nothing will ever happen between us.'

'Then why bother? Where's the return on your investment?'

'Can't I just enjoy spending time with you?'

'Yes, if that's all,' said Katie, 'but I don't think it is.'

'That's a little presumptuous, isn't it?' asked Mike.

Katie shrugged. 'It's just what I see,' she said, 'that's all. The way you look at me sometimes.'

'Don't you like me looking at you?' asked Mike.

'Yes, I do, but not if it's going to lead to . . . complications. I don't want us to fall out over it.'

'We won't,' said Mike. 'I promise you.'

'But you should be off with someone else,' said Katie, 'someone who can give you what I can't.'

'You mean sex?'

'I mean, someone who can be close to you in a way that I can't.'

'I don't want to be close to anyone else,' said Mike. 'I'm in love with you.'

'Yes, I know,' said Katie, 'and I love you – in my own way. It'd kill me if . . . if we had to be apart, but that's just it – we can't stay together because this thing will never go away.'

'It might, with time.'

'No, Mike, it'll never go away. I'll never be close to anyone in that way – physically, I mean. And if you're hoping that one day maybe, then eventually it'll drive you crazy, and you'll start to hate me.'

'And you can't tell me why?' asked Mike.

'No,' said Katie.

They sat in silence for a while.

'I even love you partly because you never ask me why,' said Katie. 'But I can't tell you, and this will never change.'

Mike looked out over the water.

'That's pretty final,' he said after a minute or so.

'I'm sorry, Mike.'

'And if I'm good?' he asked. 'If I promise not to hope, can we still be friends?'

'You know we can,' said Katie, 'if that's what you want.'

'Well,' he said, and smiled. 'I'd better learn to give up hope.'

But of course it killed him, and that was how, or why, over the next two years, Mike came up with the Vegas Plan.

By the time of their finals it was obvious that Katie was going to go into investment banking, in London though and not in Manchester. It was equally obvious that Mike wasn't; he had nothing definite in the pipeline, only that he was going to move back to Belfast for a while. Katie knew Mike would land on his feet, whatever he chose to do, and she suspected there was more for him in Belfast than he was letting on about. That left Bruno alone in Manchester – another factor in Mike coming up with the Plan.

'I want the three of us to do Vegas,' he said. 'One final trip together to really set us up for the future.'

Katie and Mike were in the White Horse. It was beginning to feel like the end of things. The buzz wasn't the same on a Saturday night; the resident DJ had been replaced by a succession of bands that provided a cover for more and more drug dealing, and this was destroying the pub. It was one thing to opt out of society, but the White Horse was no longer the happy place it used to be. In the past year the mood had changed to match that of the country as a whole. It was impossible to believe that Thatcher's war in the Falklands had resulted in her winning a landslide election; she'd be around for a few more years, and you could tell she was just itching to finish what she'd started. Well, it suited some people obviously, but it didn't suit most of the customers in the White Horse.

'Mike,' said Katie, 'when are you going to learn? You're never going to win a fortune in Vegas. Besides, I don't even have a passport.'

'Well, apply for one,' said Mike, 'because we're going – I have funding.'

'What do you mean – you have funding?' asked Katie.

'It's not worth our while,' said Mike, 'unless we have enough money to stick around for the really big hands, so I've found a partner to help bankroll the trip.'

'Who? And is Bruno going?'

'Yes,' said Mike, 'Bruno's going; he's a major reason for doing this.'

'You mean to soften the blow that you won't be around from now on?'

'And neither will you,' said Mike. 'He'll miss you too.'

'And you're feeling guilty about leaving him,' said Katie.

'Aren't you?'

'No, not at all. I'll be happy never to see him again.'

'You don't mean that,' said Mike.

'I certainly do,' said Katie. 'And I think that secretly you're relieved too, and that's why you feel guilty. Who have you found to bankroll a trip to Vegas?'

'Remember the Chinese casino in town that we were thrown out of?'

'How could I forget?' asked Katie.

'Well, I went back to them and explained the card-counting thing. They knew we were watching the cards but they didn't understand the maths.'

'And now they do?'

'Yes,' said Mike, 'and I've persuaded them to invest in this trip.'

'So whatever we win,' asked Katie, 'we have to give right back to them?'

'They want a fifty per cent return on their money.'

'Fifty per cent! We'll never do that; the best we ever made was about thirty.'

'But we've never had access to these kinds of funds before.'

'How much?'

'A hundred grand.'

'They're giving you a hundred grand to gamble with in Las Vegas?' asked Katie. 'And you have to come home with a hundred and fifty?'

'I'm not coming home,' said Mike, 'at least not to Manchester. But I do hope to pay them back, yes. I think they'd find me, even in Belfast.'

'But what security have you given them?'

'The magazine,' said Mike. 'If they don't get their hundred and fifty then I sign the magazine over to them. I could simply have sold my part of the magazine but it wasn't enough and, besides, I needed them to get the money into the country. You can't just walk into the States with that kind of money on you.'

'So what, you meet a contact who hands you over the money?'

'And who keeps an eye on me while I'm in Vegas,' said Mike. 'And of course who I give the one-fifty back to when we're done.'

'But what if you lose?' asked Katie. 'Or, what if you don't win that amount?'

Katie stopped and did the maths in her head. She looked at Mike.

'You have more than the hundred grand from the Chinese,' she said. 'You've sold the magazine anyway. Jesus Christ, Mike!'

'It's a risk, I admit,' said Mike, 'but it won't be a problem so long as I get them their one-fifty back.'

'Mike,' said Katie. 'All this, just so you can prove some card-counting theory of Eugene's might work?'

'We know it works; we've just never done it on this scale before. And you know that's not why I'm doing it. Okay, I'll admit that's part of the reason, but you know the real reason is Bruno.'

'But you don't owe him anything,' said Katie. 'He's an adult – he has to learn to look after himself.'

'You know he won't last two minutes once I'm gone from Manchester. He won't keep his job now I've sold the magazine – he's unemployable in a world of unemployment. I don't owe you anything either, but I want to do this one last thing – the three of us together.'

'Well, count me out,' said Katie. 'I've always known you were mad but this fucking takes it. You can't earn that amount in the casinos and it's not like it is here, you know – it won't be baseball bats they come at you with.'

'Vegas isn't like that anymore,' said Mike. 'It's all big business, huge corporations; they can't afford to have their customers rough-handled in public.'

'Exactly,' said Katie. 'In public! They'll take you to some back room and shoot you. You're fucking crazy, Mike.'

'They can't touch us,' said Mike. 'What we're doing isn't illegal. And if there's any trouble, we just walk – with our winnings, of course.'

'But don't you think they're wise to card counting over there too?' asked Katie. 'And they have much better monitoring systems – hidden cameras, everything!'

'That's why I need you and Bruno to help play the tables,' said Mike. 'You two can distract them before I step up with the big money.'

'No,' said Katie. 'You can forget about me; I won't do it.'

They sat in silence for a while, their own silence amidst the noise of the pub. Katie knew this was as much about her as it was about Bruno; it was Mike's way of coping with it coming to an end. He'd spent four years trying to reach Katie and now he was accepting defeat. Well, if he couldn't help her in that way, at least he could set her up with some money – he could always do that. She wouldn't have been surprised to learn that Mike intended splitting the money equally between her and Bruno.

'You don't have to prove anything, Mike,' she said. 'You're right – you don't owe me a thing. In fact, you've done more for me than I had any right to expect. But we both know – and Bruno knows – that we each have to make our own way from here.'

Katie knew that she and Bruno could quite easily lose it out there, alone in the world, and that Mike hoped somehow to be always there for them. But it was unrealistic to believe he could protect them forever.

'I'll get some drinks,' said Katie, and went up to the bar. When she returned, Mike had placed two magazines on the table, one his own and the other a university medical periodical.

'What are these?' asked Katie.

'Would it help if I told you the casinos were only a part of what I have in mind?' said Mike.

Katie looked at the two magazines.

'What?' she asked.

'Here,' said Mike, and pointed to the university periodical. 'This article on research being carried out at the university, funded by Halibro.'

'I've never heard of them.'

'I'm not surprised – they're an American pharmaceutical firm.'

'From San Diego?' asked Katie. The article mentioned similar research into heart disease in San Diego. 'What of them?'

'Well, the research doesn't exist.'

'So, why the article?' asked Katie. 'And why follow it up in your own magazine?' Mike's piece – written by one of his staff – was presented as a scoop of investigative reporting. 'Won't the company simply deny it?'

'They already have,' said Mike.

'So what's the point?'

'No point, unless someone starts investing large sums of money in Halibro, and then the more they deny it, the more people will think it's true.'

'And their share price will rise – '

'From a current low of just below two dollars per share,' said Mike.

'But nobody's going to find these articles,' said Katie. 'They're too obscure for the American stock market to care about.'

'You know as well as I do that if there's a large enough investment from somewhere then traders will find out why.'

'And this is what you intend to do with the hundred thousand, or two hundred thousand?' asked Katie.

'A bit of both, actually,' said Mike, and smiled. 'I want to increase our stake money in the casinos, and then shock the stock market into reacting.'

'You're mad!'

'I know, but it's so much more fun than being sane.'

'Seriously, Mike. You'll never trade again – or they could arrest you. What if the share price doesn't rise?'

'It will,' said Mike, 'you know it will. People are so greedy, and by then I'll have sold my shares and left the country.'

'You're mad,' said Katie again. 'They'll never let you back in the States.'

Mike shrugged. 'I was only born there,' he said. 'I've

no particular ties to the States, but my citizenship does allow me to own shares in their stock market.'

'Everything about you is crazy,' said Katie. 'How can you be a citizen of three countries? It's impossible!'

Mike smiled. 'It's too good not to try, isn't it?'

3

Katie smiled at the thought of what she was doing: driving a Lincoln convertible from Phoenix to Las Vegas.

She'd come a long way. She hadn't been entirely truthful when she told Mike when they'd first met that she'd never been out of Manchester, but she wasn't going to mention her annual trip to Blackpool for fear he might understand that she'd once been in care. This though – this was something different, and it was a measure of how much she'd achieved since leaving care at the age of eighteen. Six years later and she had a first-class degree in law, a job lined up for the end of the summer in London and – if this trip went according to Mike's plan – she was about to become financially independent for the rest of her life.

The moment wasn't entirely perfect. She wouldn't have chosen to have Bruno as a passenger in the car, for example; it would have been nice to be with Mike or, even better, alone. And she wouldn't necessarily have chosen this destination for her first trip to America, but then she wouldn't have been here at all if it wasn't for Mike, so here she was.

Las Vegas was the obvious destination for Mike, but

it took him the four years of college before he got there. He was itching to try out Eugene's card-counting theory in Vegas, but couldn't before he was twenty-one. It killed Mike to wait. He'd often been refused entry into casinos in Manchester – some had a door policy of twenty-one rather than eighteen, and he still looked very young to be out gambling. Unlike Katie, who was a couple of years older than most of their class, Mike was a year younger.

'Maybe that's why they sometimes call blackjack twenty-one,' suggested Katie.

'Very funny,' said Mike. 'It must be wonderful to be so mature and grown-up.'

Mike hadn't been able to let go of the idea that the casinos could be beaten, that it was possible to take their money by using his brain. If any one thing had dominated his time in college then it was this idea, yet to be fair Mike hadn't allowed it to take over his life. He too was about to graduate – not with the same scarily high marks as Katie, but it was a law degree all the same. Mike had too many wide-ranging interests and ideas for gambling to have become an obsession. Yet he knew, and Katie knew, that he'd never rest until he'd tried it in Vegas.

Well, thought Katie, Mike's time had come. He was about to find out if it could be done.

The three of them – Katie, Mike and Bruno – flew together to Newark and spent a few days in Atlantic City. The idea was to become accustomed to the gambling scene in the States; they made a little money, but viewed it as a holiday. From there they flew separately on internal flights – Katie and Bruno to Phoenix, where they hired the car as a couple, and Mike to Vegas.

'From the moment we leave Newark,' said Mike, 'the fewer connections they make between us, the better. You and Bruno check into the MGM Grand and I'll see you at the tables.'

They'd chosen the MGM Grand because it was due to close down, or relocate, in a year or so, and Mike thought their surveillance systems might be less sophisticated than some of the newer hotels. Katie and Bruno were to play the tables and signal to Mike when the count was good; this way Mike didn't waste time and money on playing losing hands. They were also to act as a distraction – Bruno was to make as much trouble as he could, playing the part of the unhappy loser, and Katie was to be Bruno's long-suffering girlfriend. Katie and Bruno were to bet with only small amounts, so the priming of the tables would actually cost them relatively little – for all Bruno's noise and complaints. Mike was to check in separately to a motel out by the airport in Vegas, and they were all to meet up there once they'd finished playing; there was no way Mike was hanging around the MGM Grand having taken so much of their money. Katie and Bruno were to act pissed at losing and check out early; they hoped that with over two thousand rooms in the hotel, nobody was likely to notice, let alone care.

That was the plan and that was how Katie came to

be on the highway from Phoenix to Vegas. The sun was scorching her arms but it seemed crazy not to have the top down. She looked across at Bruno; his skin seemed to be fine, as though it suited the sun. He wore a simple black T-shirt and Katie had to admit he looked good – if only he wasn't wearing a huge cowboy hat down over his face. Even this though seemed to make sense in the sun and she envied him his ease with the heat. She pulled the car over to the side of the highway and the sound of the gravel beneath the tyres disturbed Bruno. He pushed the hat up with a single finger and looked across at Katie.

'I'm burning in the sun,' said Katie. 'I need to put some more lotion on my arms.'

As the car stopped, Katie became aware of the silence. But then she realized it wasn't the silence she'd noticed, but the sounds of the desert. She was in a foreign country a long way from home, and she was alone with Bruno. While they were travelling, the motion of the car had reassured Katie that this was simply the next stage of Mike's plan, but she felt isolated out here, and didn't particularly like it.

Katie opened the car door and stepped out onto the perfect surface of the road. There were no cars visible in the heat haze hanging over the perfectly straight line of the highway. She opened the boot of the car and reached into her bag for the lotion. She poured it along the length of both arms and then across her shoulders. As she rubbed it in she caught Bruno looking at her in the rear-view mirror. She wiped the remaining lotion on her hands across her face and fore-head. She pulled out a light long-sleeved shirt and put it on, though it was clingy and uncomfortable on her arms.

'What's the point of putting lotion on if you're going to cover yourself up?' asked Bruno, when Katie got back into the car.

Katie started the engine and pulled away, without turning to look behind her.

'The point is,' she said, 'it's what I choose to do.'

Katie thought they'd have little difficulty with their act of not getting on too well together.

'Those cactuses are crazy,' said Bruno, looking at the strange plants scattered across the desert. They passed by the occasional billboard, and huge boulders that looked as though they'd been thrown from the sky.

'Cacti,' said Katie. 'The plural of cactus is cacti.'

She drove on for a while, and turned to look at Bruno.

'Why do you do that?' she asked. 'You know the plural of cactus is cacti, but you have to say it wrong – just to be some . . . I don't know, like there was some value in appearing more stupid than you really are.'

Bruno did his finger with the hat thing again.

'I don't know,' he said. 'Why do you have to correct me? Just to be some . . . I don't know, like it makes you somehow better than me?'

Bruno slid down into his seat and pushed the hat back down over his face.

'Suarro,' he said from beneath the hat. 'That's what they're called – they're suarro cacti.'

Katie drove the rest of the journey in silence.

The noise in the casino was so overpowering that Katie didn't believe the owners of the MGM Grand were aware of everything that went on in their hotel, but Mike had assured her that they were.

'Don't be distracted by the gaming machines,' he'd told her.

Katie understood what Mike meant once she and Bruno reached the quieter area of the card tables. It was hard to stay focused when Katie knew that every move she made was watched and recorded from above. Okay, so they couldn't keep track of every player all the time, but they could focus in on whomever they liked. The glass ceiling concealed a series of walkways that ran above the casino; security watchers looked down on the tables, and a series of cameras fed back to the main observation room deep within the hotel. Mike had told Katie repeatedly not to look up at the ceiling, however tempted she might be. And what did Katie do when she first walked in the room? Looked up at the ceiling, of course.

Bruno, to be fair, played his part to perfection – a loud, ignorant first-timer, kicking up a fuss about losing what for this casino was a pathetically small amount of money. His behaviour made it easier for Katie to play her role. She didn't know how much of the antipathy she felt was towards Bruno, or the character he had become. The longer the day went on, the more repugnant Bruno was to Katie.

By early evening Katie had had enough. She hated the unreal world of the casino. She hated the oxygen she knew they pumped into the room to stop her feeling tired. She hated the complimentary food and drinks; she didn't want to be spoilt while the casino took her money. This wasn't the America that Katie longed to see, and she hated Mike for bringing her here.

Katie looked over to where a crowd had gathered around Mike's table. She knew what this meant: Mike's winnings were large enough to attract the attention of players from surrounding tables. It wouldn't be long before the watchers above alerted the security on the floor of the casino; Mike's time was almost up.

Katie stepped up behind Bruno and tugged at his sleeve. He shrugged her off in a temper.

'We have to go,' said Katie.

'I'm not leaving till I win my money back,' Bruno shouted.

'You can't win your money back, you idiot,' said Katie. 'You've no chips left to place another bet.'

The players at Bruno's table looked away in embarrassment. Katie tugged again at Bruno's sleeve. Bruno lashed out drunkenly behind him, and his arm caught the tray of a passing waitress, sending drinks across the floor and splashing the woman sat next to him.

'Oh, fucking hell, I'm sorry,' said Bruno, and he

reached for a paper napkin. The woman stepped away, and put up her hands in front of Bruno.

'Don't you dare touch me,' she said.

Katie walked away in disgust. She saw a security guard hold his hand to his ear, and knew he was receiving instructions from above. A man who could only have been a pit boss walked purposefully towards Mike's table. Katie moved quickly across to intercept him; she could see he was oblivious to anything else that might be happening on the gambling floor.

'Excuse me,' said Katie, and stood in the man's way. 'Could you help me, please? My husband – he's . . . I need to get him away from the tables and back to our room. I'm worried he might harm someone if I don't get him out of here.'

The pit boss listened to his earpiece as Katie spoke. He was torn between the disturbance Bruno was creating and the growing crowd at Mike's table.

'Please,' said Katie.

The pit boss couldn't simply ignore Katie; she was creating something of a stir herself. The players at Bruno's table watched her asking for help; passers-by wondered just what a woman like Katie was doing with an oaf such as Bruno.

'I can't actually stop a guest from playing at the tables, ma'am,' said the pit boss.

'Oh, for God's sake, man,' snapped Katie, and she walked back to Bruno. A huge round of applause went up from the watching crowd over at Mike's table. Bruno had his back to Katie.

'Either you come back to our room now,' said Katie, 'or you'll be sleeping alone tonight.'

There were a few laughs around the table. They wanted Bruno to be gone, but they were beginning to enjoy the show.

'Aw honey,' said Bruno. He spoke in a Texan drawl.

'Don't you "Aw honey" me!' said Katie. 'It's your choice.'

Katie turned and walked away. She heard the laughter at the table as Bruno scrambled to catch up with her.

'My hat,' he cried, and ran back, but Katie carried on walking. She could see Mike over to her left. He'd left the blackjack tables, but he didn't seem to be leaving the gambling floor. Players were congratulating him, and Mike was making a big show of carrying all his chips – but he was lingering over by the roulette tables.

I don't believe it, thought Katie.

She realized what Mike was about to do. She stopped and watched as Mike dropped his winning chips onto a roulette table. Mike's usual trick – whenever he did this – was to place them all on red, but Katie knew he could quite as easily bet everything on a single number.

Katie dropped any pretence of storming out of the casino. She couldn't see the roulette table for the crowd that had once again gathered around Mike. She stood still and waited. The pit boss and security guard were over to Katie's right; they could do nothing now that

Mike's success had become such a public show. There was a hush amongst the crowd, and Katie guessed they'd spun the wheel.

Bruno came up behind Katie, and tried to usher her towards the exit. She refused to budge.

'We have to get out of here,' Bruno said quietly.

He grabbed Katie's arm, but she shook him off. Katie had to wait to see the outcome of Mike's play.

'Katie,' said Bruno.

Another loud cheer went up around Mike, and the noise released the tension in the room. Katie and Bruno walked off the floor and up to their room.

As Bruno shut the hotel bedroom door, Katie knew this wasn't going to go well. She could see that Bruno was still high, and when Bruno was high, bad things happened around him.

'Oh yes!' said Bruno. He dramatically rested the back of his head against the door. 'We did it! We fucking did it, man!'

This was always going to be the difficult moment in Mike's plan – when Katie was left alone with Bruno in private. She knew what Bruno's mind would turn to; he never stopped thinking about it anyway, so why should he stop now? He was too high to expect anything else.

'You mean Mike did it,' she said.

'Mike did it, you did it – we all did it. We're a fucking team,' said Bruno, 'that's what we are.'

Some team, thought Katie.

'Well, it's done now,' she said. 'Mike proved it could be done.'

'You were fucking great, Katie,' said Bruno. 'They didn't have a clue, did they?'

'And do you think they bug the hotel rooms?' asked Katie.

'What?'

'Do you think they record the conversations of their guests? Or watch their reaction on closed-circuit TV?'

'What do you mean?' asked Bruno.

'I mean,' said Katie, 'that you and I have just lost a fair bit of money down there – and we come back here and celebrate?'

'I dunno,' said Bruno, and then, 'No-o. They can't do that. Do you think? No, they'd have laws.'

'I'd say they could do whatever they like,' said Katie, 'so long as nobody finds out. They've just been taken for a lot of money; my guess is they'd like to know how.'

'They can't arrest you for counting cards,' said Bruno.

'But they don't like it,' said Katie, 'and they don't believe it can be done.'

'But it's going to be Mike they're watching, and he's left the hotel.'

'We hope,' said Katie.

'We know,' said Bruno. 'We watched him leave. Come on, Katie, loosen up – we've done it.'

He threw his ridiculous ten-gallon hat across the room and strode over to Katie. He reached for her right hand and, although she stepped back, he pulled her towards the bedroom.

Katie resisted as the panic hit her inside. She knew this scene; she knew the inevitability of this scene, but had completely underestimated the strength of Bruno's presumption.

'What are you doing?' she asked. She tried desperately to keep her voice at a level pitch.

'Come on,' said Bruno again. 'You can drop the act now – we've done it. All we have to do now is get the hell out of Dodge – by which I mean we check the fuck out of this grotesque hotel – and fuck off back to Manchester. Nice Guy Mike isn't going to stick one over on us, certainly not on me, and he's too smitten to cheat on you. So I say we go in there' – Bruno indicated the bedroom with a nod of his head – 'and we fuck each other's brains out like I've wanted to ever since we first met.'

Bruno pulled Katie towards him and put his arms around her waist. He still held her right hand and this forced Katie's arm up behind her back.

Katie prayed the panic wasn't written on her face. How had this happened so quickly? Less than ten seconds to lose a lifetime of control? Was that all it took?

Katie tried moving her arm and felt the strength in Bruno's grip. Would he really force her against her will? Katie doubted it, though if Bruno knew their happy threesome was at an end, then why not – nothing to lose at the last-chance saloon? Katie looked into

Bruno's eyes but she saw no clues – he was high. Of course he was high; Bruno was always high. He was high on the drink and the oxygen downstairs, high on the performance of the past few hours – although it couldn't have taken much for Bruno to act the loud-mouthed buffoon. He was high on the money – Bruno was just plain high, and nothing Katie could say would reach him.

'You've been fucking asking for it for years,' said Bruno, 'hiding behind Mike all that time. But you're not with Mike, are you? So why not?'

'I haven't – ' began Katie, but she stopped and closed her eyes. Katie's own act from downstairs – the frosty bitch partner – gave her a few seconds' grace at most.

Please let me get out of this, she thought.

Was it so wrong not to be with someone? To never have sex?

There was safety at first in all their friends at college, but as the numbers had dwindled it became harder for Katie to hide. So she used Mike, who was too sweet either to notice or to complain. Katie used Mike to pass for normal – to pass for what the likes of Bruno would consider normal.

Katie let her head drop to Bruno's chest, and relaxed her body into his arms.

'Bruno,' she said, 'I've thought of this too, believe me. How many times are we alone and away from Mike? Just this one time – and you're right about Mike; I'm not with him at all.'

'I knew it!' said Bruno. He released his grip on Katie and paced across the room. Bruno let Katie go without a second thought, because he knew he could grab her again whenever he liked.

Katie took her opportunity.

'Believe me, Bruno,' she said, 'I've thought about this – about us – and I want it the same as you. But not here, not while we're still in this hotel, not while we're still in the game.'

'Where then?' asked Bruno. 'And when?'

'The desert,' said Katie. 'I had this idea – we meet Mike now to say goodbye, and then we drive back to Phoenix. I was going to suggest we pull over from the highway, out in the desert, under the stars – away from all this. Out there with just the two of us – that's how I'd pictured it. Maybe I was just being silly,' she added.

'Are you serious?' asked Bruno. 'I mean – '

'Of course,' said Katie. 'Do you really think it hadn't crossed my mind? Out alone in the desert with you? Of course I'd thought about it – that's why I was so irritable this morning. But I want it to be right. We still have to get out of here; we still have to do our leaving act together. Everything we can do to distract them from Mike, the safer it is for all of us. I'd say he's pretty lonely right now.'

'You're right,' said Bruno. 'You're right. We've got to be professional about this.'

As though being professional included the promise of a fuck in the desert, thought Katie, but it worked.

Bruno grabbed their cases – they hadn't unpacked because they knew they wouldn't be staying the night. Katie kicked off the dress shoes she'd worn down at the casino, and changed back into the comfortable driving shoes from earlier in the day.

The desk clerk at reception wasn't surprised when Katie and Bruno asked to check out the hotel; he was too busy to care.

'I'll have to charge you for the full night's stay though, ma'am,' he said to Katie.

'I'll bet you do,' said Bruno. 'As if you haven't taken enough of our money already. And stop calling her ma'am, can't you? Does she look like your ma'am?'

Katie paid the bill in cash.

'Can we offer you this memento of your stay with us?' the clerk asked Katie. He held up a metal replica of the hotel. 'It's a model of the MGM Grand.'

'Is it worth anything?' asked Bruno.

'Well,' said the clerk, 'we are moving to a brand new building, so who knows – maybe in a year or two?'

'No, thanks,' said Katie, but Bruno reached across her.

'We'll take it,' he said. 'You fucking owe us big time, man. Come on, let's get out of here.' He grabbed the model and picked up the bags. 'Where's our fucking car? You! Yeah, you, ya little prick! Go and fetch our car!'

Katie had to admit Bruno was good, and she was relieved to be getting out of here.

*

When they met up with Mike, Katie relaxed a little, though she knew she still had to get to Phoenix.

'The roulette wasn't part of the plan,' she said to Mike.

'Oh, you saw that, did you?'

'It was stupid,' said Katie.

'What was stupid?' asked Bruno.

'Mike placing all his chips on the roulette table.'

'I won, didn't I?' said Mike. 'That doubled our winnings in one stroke.'

'But you could have lost everything,' said Katie, 'including our stake money.'

'But I didn't,' said Mike, 'and now we stand to make a fortune. I've paid off the Chinese, so we're in the clear – everything from here on in is pure profit.'

'But what if you'd lost?'

'But I didn't,' repeated Mike. 'Besides, it helped me get out of there. They can't be seen to have a problem with someone winning at the roulette table, and it took their attention away from the cards. They cashed in my chips without blinking. Come on, let's order some drinks and food – I'm starving.'

'I don't know why we can't just leave now,' said Bruno. 'I mean, forget about the second part of the plan.'

Bruno knew why Mike was staying in the States and he understood the potential of what Mike had in mind. He also knew it was illegal, but this wasn't what was bothering Bruno – now they had some money, Bruno would have settled for less and the chance of seeing Mike again.

'Fuck it!' he said. 'I'm going to powder my nose. I

don't want any food — would you order me a beer? Several beers, actually.' He picked up the metal model of the MGM Grand; it was tacky but Bruno had taken a liking to it.

'Is he okay?' Mike asked Katie, once Bruno had left the table. 'How the hell did he get hold of drugs? I didn't know he had any money on him.'

'Is he okay?' asked Katie. 'Yes and no; I wish we were all going home together.'

'So do I,' said Mike, 'but this next thing will take at least a couple of weeks to happen. And you should be thousands of miles away; even this dinner is risky.'

'You've a hell of a way of dumping a girl,' said Katie. She rested her hand on Mike's arm. Katie knew it was she who had made the choice.

Bruno returned to the table and Katie pulled away from Mike. They ordered beer and food and sat silently while their table was laid. The waitress went to move Bruno's model to one side of his place setting, but he stopped her.

'Just leave the knives and forks, can't you?' he said rudely.

'That thing sure is heavy,' said the waitress. She brought the beers and then left them alone.

'Fucking hell, Bruno,' said Katie. 'What's wrong with you?'

Bruno seemed morose, which was worrying given the amount of cocaine he'd just snorted. Mike tried to make small talk, but it was turning very much into their last supper together.

'You think I'm pretty stupid, don't you?' Bruno said

to Mike. 'You think I don't know what you're doing here? Hiding behind some scam when it's obvious you just don't want to see me anymore.'

'Bruno, that's not – '

'I wish you had the honesty to at least admit it. And you . . .' He turned to Katie. 'You with your talk of a fuck in the desert – you were pretty fucking smart to get me out of that hotel bedroom.'

'No, I – '

'Well, fuck you both is what I say.'

He picked up a fork from the table and stabbed it into his cheekbone, just below his eye.

'Bruno!' said Mike.

'Oh Jesus,' said Katie.

Bruno dragged the fork down his cheek and stared, first at Katie and then at Mike. He threw the fork down on the table and pushed away his chair. He picked up the model of the MGM Grand.

'Enjoy your meal,' he said, and left the room.

'Now what?' asked Katie, as the waitress brought their food.

'Do you think I should go after him?' asked Mike.

'You can do whatever the fuck you think is best,' said Katie, 'but I've had it with him. I'm going to eat my meal and then drive to Phoenix. He's an adult; he can look after himself.'

'But that's just it, isn't it?' said Mike. 'He can't look after himself.'

'He's got a plane ticket and a passport – if he's not on the plane, then tough!'

'But how will he get to Phoenix if you don't take him in the car?'

'It's time to start letting go,' said Katie. 'You knew he was going to be a disaster on his own – well, he's just started early is all.'

'This is all my fault,' said Mike. 'I should never have tried to include him in this trip.'

'You should never have tried to include him – full stop!' said Katie. 'The guy's a total loser and has been since day one. You don't owe Bruno anything, Mike; you never have done, so stop taking responsibility for his actions.'

This was where their every discussion about Bruno had always ended. Katie concentrated on her food, but there was so much on the plate, it was obscene. She lost her appetite.

'He won't be able to cope,' said Mike after a while. He pushed his plate to one side.

'You can't help him, Mike,' said Katie, 'just like you can't help me. The best thing you can do is walk away.'

'Is that really how you feel – about us?' asked Mike.

'I think if you don't let go then it will end up driving you crazy and making you very, very unhappy. That goes for Bruno too – we're a pair of hopeless cases that you're better off without. Go back to Belfast, Mike, and marry your sweetheart; make her happy at least.'

Mike looked away, down to one side of the table.

'I don't want to live my life without you,' he said.

'I know you don't,' said Katie, 'but you're going to have to – for your own good.' She stood up. 'I'm leaving now, Mike. I think you can pay for the meal, all things considered. And if Bruno turns up, put him in a cab and take the fare out of his earnings.' She thought this was for the best anyway – that way she avoided the journey through the desert with Bruno. 'Thank you,' she said, one last time, 'for everything.'

Katie walked out of the restaurant and didn't look back. It seemed like the only thing to do.

When she reached the car, she was disappointed to see Bruno asleep in the passenger seat. He cradled the MGM Grand in his arms. Katie could see where the blood had dried on his cheek.

'Bruno,' she said, but he didn't stir. She considered going back to Mike at the restaurant and then decided against it; she had to handle things on her own from now on. Bruno might sleep the whole way, and the journey to Phoenix could pass off without incident. Once they reached the airport, Bruno could do as he pleased. If he created a scene and they refused to allow him on the plane, then that was nothing to Katie. At least this way she could do Mike the favour of freeing him from Bruno.

Katie opened the car door. Bruno was leaning heavily over towards her and she pushed him away, over to the other side of the car. Bruno's head rolled onto the passenger door with a thump, but he didn't wake up. Whatever it was Bruno thought he'd been taking, it certainly wasn't cocaine – he was out of it. The last thing Katie wanted was for Bruno to need medical assistance, but he was breathing regularly enough and didn't look to be in any danger. She turned on the engine, put the car in drive and set off for Phoenix. She drove too quickly over a ramp of some sort as she joined the highway, and Bruno's head jerked forward onto his chest. Katie reached across with her right arm; she pulled at Bruno's hair so his head rested back between the headrest and the side of the car.

Katie felt easier once she was on the highway. It was a smooth road and there was no reason for Bruno to be disturbed. Although it was dark, the highway was busy enough with traffic, much busier in fact than it had been during the day. Katie felt relatively secure. It was a beautiful car to drive and she could quite easily have travelled much faster in comfort, but she kept to a level 55 mph; she didn't want to attract the attention of the occasional patrol cars she saw pass her by in the opposite direction. Although the air grew noticeably cooler as she drove out into the desert, it was still warm enough to keep the top down. It was a pleasant sensation to be in control of such a large, powerful car and to sense the expanse of desert surrounding her. Earlier in the day the desert had been too hot to enjoy, and Katie had been nervous of what lay ahead in Vegas. Now, the job was done and she had the measure of the car; she was unlikely ever to make this journey again, so why not relax and enjoy the drive?

She travelled for two hours before Bruno stirred. Katie looked over and she could see he was having difficulty breathing in that position. She considered reaching over to adjust the way his head was resting, but he opened his eyes. Bruno looked out at the road-side passing him by, and then across at Katie.

'Where are we?'

'Just outside Phoenix,' said Katie. They still had a good distance to go but she wanted Bruno sedate and quiet. 'I'll give you a shout when we're almost there, if you like.'

'Mike,' he said. Bruno seemed to be having trouble coming round. He looked at the model that he cradled in his arms and lifted it onto the top of the dashboard. He wiped some dribble from the side of his mouth.

'Mike's back in Vegas,' said Katie. 'You were asleep in the car when I came out of the restaurant, and we couldn't wake you. What were you taking to knock you out like that?'

'Not what I thought I was taking,' said Bruno, 'that's for sure. I feel like shit.'

'There's a bottle of water behind your seat. You might wash your face too, while you're at it.'

Bruno adjusted the rear-view mirror to look at his face, and closed his eyes when he saw what he'd done to himself.

'Fucking idiot,' he said, and shook his head.

'You said it,' said Katie.

Bruno reached for the bottle of water, took a few mouthfuls and then poured some into his cupped hand. He splashed it across the side of his face and winced at the pain. The wound didn't look much better for being cleaned.

'I hope they let you on the plane looking like that,' said Katie.

'I'm not getting on the plane,' said Bruno.

'So what do you intend to do,' asked Katie, 'stay here forever?'

'There's nothing back in Manchester for me,' said Bruno. 'Once the money comes through from Mike, I reckon I can start a new life here.'

'They have immigration laws, Bruno. They know you're in the country and when they find you, they'll throw you out of the country.'

'I'm not going back to Manchester,' said Bruno.

'Fine,' said Katie, 'whatever you say, but I'm driving to the airport and returning this car. I'm not going to leave any loose ends for them to trace me back to Mike.'

'You're a fucking ruthless bitch, aren't you?' said Bruno. 'Now you have your money, you just dump Mike and never see him again – is that it?'

'Don't start, Bruno; you know that was what we agreed. If you didn't like the plan, you shouldn't have agreed to come.'

'Like I had a choice,' said Bruno. He readjusted the mirror and Katie reached up to correct her rear-view vision. Bruno touched her cheek with his fingertips.

'When are we stopping?' he asked.

'We're not stopping,' said Katie. 'I told you – we're almost there.'

'I mean when are we stopping to have sex?'

'You're joking, aren't you?' said Katie, but already she was scared.

'You promised,' said Bruno. 'It was part of the plan – you can't go back on it now.'

'Yes,' said Katie, 'but that was before you stabbed yourself with a fork and nearly gouged your eye out. Besides, we've passed by where I was thinking of stopping. We're almost in Phoenix now; there's nowhere here suitable to pull over.'

'We could do it in the car,' said Bruno. 'Switch to cruise control – why aren't you using cruise control anyway if you're going to stick to the one speed? Come on, Katie, let's fuck.'

Katie drove on. She could see where the sky was bright from the lights of Phoenix, but they were still some distance away. If she just drove on there was very little Bruno could do. But then he reached over and put his hand on her thigh and she froze. She felt as though the blood in her head was blocking her ears and her eyes too, somehow; she was blind with anger. She was unable to speak; she couldn't even tell Bruno to take away his hand. No one had ever touched Katie there and now this, this . . . thing that she didn't even understand how it was a part of her life – this thing was touching her. Bruno moved his hand up and around Katie's thigh and she thought she was going to be sick.

She was conscious of the car travelling at speed, and of the lines on the road moving across the car, and the rougher sound and feel of the gravel as the car veered off the road.

'Whoa!' shouted Bruno and laughed, and he let go of Katie's thigh to grab the wheel. 'Slow down,' he said, and tried to keep the car from leaving the highway completely.

Katie was aware of Bruno laughing, but wasn't aware of what he was saying.

Bruno tried to lift Katie's foot off the gas pedal with his left hand and guide the wheel with his right. Each time he looked down at her feet, he lost any sense of direction for the car. 'Fucking brake, can't you?' He laughed and tried to push down the brake pedal with his hand.

Katie let go of the wheel and looked down at the top of Bruno's head. She reached over to the dash-board and picked up the metal model of the MGM Grand. She brought it down heavily on the back of Bruno's neck. It made a dull thump it was so heavy. Bruno slumped forward and down. The car shook over the rougher terrain and leaned at such an acute angle that it was in danger of tipping over. Still holding the model, Katie grabbed the wheel again and guided the car onto level ground. She couldn't get her feet to the brake pedal because Bruno's head and upper body were between her legs, but the car gradually slowed down. Twice Katie had to turn sharply to avoid huge boulders that appeared in the bright headlights, and then flashed on by. The freakishly large cacti reared up like cartoon jokes – like silent observers – before disappearing again into the desert night. When the car came to a stop, Katie switched off the engine and turned off the lights. She closed her eyes and waited.

It was the weight of the model in her hand that brought Katie round. She replaced it on the dashboard. She let her eyes become accustomed to the darkness; she could have switched on the headlights again, but they only illuminated the immediate direction in which they were pointing and made the rest of the night seem doubly dark. This way she could at least get a feel for where she was, without attracting the attention of the traffic she saw passing by on the highway. Katie reached down and felt the back of Bruno's head, expecting it to be a sticky mess, but it wasn't too bad – just still and heavy. She pulled at Bruno's hair but couldn't get his body out from around her feet. She managed to free her own legs and stepped out of the car onto the rough ground of the open desert. Once she was standing, Katie could reach in and grab Bruno properly by the shoulders. She lifted him first onto her own seat and then pushed him upright back into the passenger seat. She rested and listened for Bruno's breathing, and tried to think what best to do.

She could drive back to the highway, but she couldn't ask for help – there'd be too many questions. Or drive on to Phoenix, and decide what to do once she reached the airport? There'd be more questions in Phoenix, and delays, and Katie's fate would depend on Bruno pulling through. She could empty him out of the car and dump him here in the desert – she didn't care if he lived or died; he was nothing to her now. Katie didn't really know how hard she'd hit him. She knew she had to feel for a pulse to make sure, but she didn't want to know what the lack of a pulse would tell her.

She walked around the car and opened the passenger door. She pulled Bruno from the car to the ground – a much harder job than she had thought because his feet got jammed between the seat and the doorframe. She grabbed him under the arms and pulled him away from the car towards a large boulder shape she could make out behind her. She dropped him by the boulder and stood upright to get her bearings. From the lights of the occasional passing car or truck, Katie figured out that the highway curved gradually around her present position. She pulled Bruno round to the blind side of the boulder and rolled him in tight beneath an overhang. She peered into the darkness behind her and could sense nothing except open desert, but of course morning might come and there'd be a huge diner there or anything. The sky was full of stars, but they gave off little or no light to help Katie see into the night.

She reached into Bruno's pockets, looking for his ticket and passport, but she found nothing – perhaps they were still in his bag, or in the glove compartment of the car? Katie came back from around the boulder and for a second panicked as she thought she'd lost sight of the car but then she made it out over to her right. She walked over and reached into the glove compartment – nothing there. She walked back to the boot of the car and went through Bruno's bag – nothing. What had he done with them? Sold them, or swapped them for drugs?

Katie stood by the car. So long as there was no identification on Bruno, she could think of nothing to tie him to her. She wanted to be safe in Manchester before any connection was made between them. She could easily dispose of his bag when she came to a suitable spot – hell, she could throw it out in the desert and no one would care. His passport was a different matter, but whatever he'd done with it, Katie would be long gone before anyone came looking. She was conscious of the time – if she stayed here much longer she'd be cutting it fine for her flight. She slammed down the boot of the car and walked round to the driver's door. Katie saw the model of the MGM Grand still on the dashboard and reached across to grab it. She went back to the far side of the boulder, stumbling twice on the smaller rocks and stones beneath her feet. She heard Bruno move on the desert floor.

'Fucking hell, Katie,' he said, 'what did you do?'

Katie leant in to where Bruno was lying beneath the boulder. She swung the model high above her and crashed it down onto Bruno's head.

'You don't ever touch me there,' she said. 'Do you hear me?' She swung and hit him again. 'Never!'

Bruno's leg twitched for a second and then he was still, but Katie hit him again. She hit him again and again and again.

THREE

I

Margaret Maguire lay in bed and listened and waited for the sound of the front door to be closed. Once she knew she was alone in the house, she pushed herself up into a sitting position and picked up the cup of tea her husband Mike had made before leaving. It was six thirty in the morning.

'I'll be home between eight and nine this evening,' Mike had said.

'Will you have eaten?' She spoke without opening her eyes, sleepily, and into her pillow.

'I'll eat on the plane.'

'Will that be enough for you?'

'Possibly not,' said Mike, 'but I'll grab something else if I need to when I get home – don't wait for me.'

'I'll see,' said Margaret. 'How I feel at the time, I mean.' Her alternative was to eat alone. 'Have a good day.'

It was too early for her to be drinking tea but Mike liked to bring her a drink in the morning, regardless of the time he was leaving. She took a sip and wrapped her hands around the cup, enjoying the heat through her fingers. She wondered what Mike might be doing. She knew he was going to Dublin but he hadn't told Margaret why, only saying that he was following up on a business idea. How many times had she heard that?

She'd given up trying to pin him down when it came to business ideas. Mike explained that if he talked about it too soon it might never come off; you had to let the idea grow, to test it privately before opening it up to public scrutiny. By public, he meant Margaret. She didn't mind so long as he provided for her and the family, and he'd certainly always done that. She knew Mike was a restless soul when it came to business; once he'd achieved something, he had to move on and find another challenge.

Like Woody Allen's shark, she thought, and smiled. Or was that a cat? And that was relationships, not business – anyway, it was too early for details like that.

When the children were little, Margaret had worried and felt vulnerable; she didn't want to be married to a chancer. She was as dependent on Mike as her young dependent children were on her, living in a city in a foreign country – whatever some might claim – away from her family and friends in Belfast. But things had gradually changed: the children grew, Manchester became her home and she knew now that, if needs be, she could manage on her own.

Margaret had recently taken again to playing a game that once had terrified her – the 'What if Mike leaves tomorrow?' game. It was a game she increasingly felt she could win, even if she upped the odds a little each time. What if she lost the house? What if it happened before she finished the training on her counselling course? It was a test to see how far as a woman she'd come from that Belfast girl. And now, of course, she knew that Mike would always be able to discover new ways of making money; it wasn't this that should have worried her at all.

So what if this was the last cup of tea Mike ever brought her? What if this morning was Margaret's last chance to see him, and she didn't even open her eyes to say goodbye? She couldn't blame Mike if he decided never to come back.

What if there was something more than business in Dublin for Mike? What exactly were the secrets he'd been keeping from her all these years?

Well, Margaret had her secrets now too.

Was that what this was all about – because she didn't know what Mike got up to, she had to get up to something herself?

Margaret closed her eyes again – the day wasn't five minutes old and already the guilt was back, at her. She took a deep breath and another sip of tea.

And what good had her own secrets done for her? She had less of an idea than ever what Mike might do with his days, and a greater reason than ever before to fear she might not be the centre of his world. She'd had to tell him anyway, tell him what she'd done, because she couldn't stand the weight of her secret any longer. Mike asked her who it was.

'Don't you want to know why?' she asked. 'Isn't why more important than who?'

'Oh right,' said Mike, 'so there's a league table, is there – a correct order in which I should be asking these things? You have rules for that as well now, do you?'

'What do you mean "rules for that as well"? What else do I have rules for?'

'Just tell me who it is, will you?'

'It's not important,' said Margaret. 'It's more important you know why.'

'But it obviously is important to me,' said Mike.

Margaret sat there in silence.

'Jesus Christ, all right then – why?' said Mike.

But in the end Margaret didn't tell him who or why. The reasons she used to justify to herself what she'd done sounded feeble when she saw the effect her words had on Mike. That he was never around? That even when Mike was home he never seemed fully there? That she'd felt redundant, useless now the kids were grown up? That she'd always feared he didn't love her, that he loved someone else?

So she got in the first blow, just to protect herself.

Margaret could see Mike was devastated. She didn't expect him to be overjoyed, but she was surprised at the extent of his upset. Part of her thought he had it coming – he'd forgotten what she meant to him, forgotten what she could do to him if she put her mind to it.

'Are you saying you've never been with another woman?' she shouted at Mike. Her aggressiveness came from her disgust at herself.

'Not since I've been with you,' he said.

'You haven't been with another woman in over twenty years?'

'No!' said Mike. 'Why – is this something you do all

the time? Or just something you think I do all the time?'

'But you're always away,' said Margaret. 'You have plenty of opportunity.'

'And because I have the opportunity, it means I must take the opportunity?'

'I don't believe you've never looked at another woman,' said Margaret.

'Of course I've looked at other women, and I've thought about it too – I've just never done anything about it.'

'Well you're a saint then,' said Margaret, 'or a liar.'

And so it went on, around and around, round after round, Margaret trying to justify what she'd done by something Mike had not.

'You just weren't there,' she said one day.

'What do you mean?' asked Mike. 'Of course I wasn't there, otherwise you wouldn't have done it. But where was I? Out earning money for you and our kids and our home, that's where. That's what I thought my role was – to provide. You certainly made that plain enough when we first got married. Where's the money coming from, Mike? What's going to happen to the business, Mike? Why do you have to change what you're doing, Mike? Jesus Christ! No one told me I had to stay at home all day so my wife could feel secure, and wouldn't feel the need to go and fuck some other bloke. No one told me that was the deal.'

'I don't mean you weren't there physically,' said Margaret. 'You were too distant, I wouldn't know where your mind would be half the time. Oh, I don't know. I don't know why I did it, okay?'

Over and over it went through Margaret's head. She put the half-drunk cup of tea down on the bedside table and lay back in the bed. She couldn't start every day in this way, couldn't go through each day beating herself up like this. What she had done she had done, but this guilt was killing her. She turned onto her side and pulled the bedclothes over her head. She was a tiny figure in the huge bed, a tiny figure in a huge bed in a huge room; a beautiful room in a beautiful house; a family home with only Margaret inside.

They moved here soon after Jack was born, Margaret heavily pregnant with their second child – another boy, whom they called Mike. They took the large front bedroom for themselves and decided the size of the room demanded a statement of a bed, a big heavy wooden bed that people could be born in and people could die in. And mothers could lie with their children in, as Margaret had, and yes, that was the happiest time of her life. She finally felt safe and secure, in her bed with her children around her, her husband out at work, earning the money to pay for their beautiful home.

So when had it stopped being enough? When had Margaret started wanting more? When did she first notice the void? Where had it come from and what had been there to fill it before? She was happy; it was tough enough at first but she was happy. Once the kids were all at school, though, she knew she had to find something new. She was a young woman still – she'd only been an adult for as long as she'd been a child. Margaret could simplify her life since school into four easy decisions: nursing, marrying Mike, moving to Manchester and having the children. She didn't regret any of them. But she was still only just turned thirty – what the hell would she do next?

Margaret had returned to nursing, encouraged by Mike and supported by Jack and Mike junior, who loved her in her uniform (as did Mike senior, but that was a different story – would it work for him now, she wondered?). It wasn't the sudden exposure to the workplace that had changed Margaret. She knew her way around the ward and she fitted right in; she was too good a nurse not to. There was no great awakening of her consciousness, no sudden dissatisfaction with her lot in life. In fact, it had very little to do with her at all and much more to do with Mike: who the hell was this person, and why had he chosen to be with her? They'd been married for over ten years before Margaret began to realize that she didn't really know Mike at all.

And now another ten years have gone by, thought Margaret.

Their house backed on to Longford Park, one of a terrace of large properties with long gardens that reached all the way to the perimeter of the park. Margaret listened to the early-morning sound of birds singing, about the only time of day they weren't drowned out by the sound of traffic. She still couldn't recognize the individual songs of particular birds. As a child she'd asked her mother to teach her, but her mother didn't know and Belfast wasn't the place to listen to birdsong on a regular basis. Margaret had wanted to know for when she had children of her own but – just like her mother before her – it was unlikely now that she'd ever learn. Not that the children ever asked her, but it would have been nice to be able to tell them.

The house had served its purpose as their family home but what was to become of it now, Margaret didn't know. Jack was settled in Leeds, if you could call working in a pub settled. And while Mike junior might occasionally turn up for a few days at a time, you wouldn't want to base your life around it; he'd inherited his father's restlessness and was currently working as a boat painter down in Cornwall. This was not a house then for a woman to be alone in; Margaret may not have known what had happened to the years as her children were growing up, but she was well aware of what was going on now. She snuggled deeper down into the bed, trying not to listen to the silence of the large empty house. Her children were gone; her husband was gone; she was alone.

They were so right to leave Belfast when they did. Margaret was surprised when Mike considered staying for a while once he'd finished his degree in Manchester – although Mike's Belfast was always very different to Margaret's. He seemed to need a few months to decide what to do next and spent it with his parents up in Hollywood, detached from reality as Margaret saw it.

She didn't understand why he hadn't taken the job with the investment bank that had sponsored him through college, but she presumed he must have his reasons. She didn't mind waiting but that was because she knew she was on her way out of there regardless. Belfast, post-hunger strikes, was a nasty little town and getting worse. She was leaving with or without Mike. There was nothing to be done with the place but to walk away.

English people were so funny when she first met them – they couldn't conceive of living in a place like Belfast, or what it must do to your head.

'It must make you very hard' was the phrase they used, but Margaret thought that if anything it was the leaving of Belfast that had made her so – hard in the sense that she prevented her emotions from getting the better of her. What could you do; how could you reason through what they'd allowed to happen? And why were those deaths any worse than any others? The only thing to do was to shut down your mind.

That autumn Mike suggested they get married and go to live in Manchester. Margaret agreed. She loved him and she believed that he loved her – he'd just taken his time to realize it – and there was no way she was staying in the North after marrying Mike. Her own family were reasonable enough, but Margaret knew what she was doing; she knew she'd rarely see them again. They didn't shun her; it was just that everybody understood the choice she was taking. This was her way out and this was the price she would pay.

On a personal level Margaret had taken a gamble on

Mike and placed herself in a vulnerable position in a foreign city. Although she was a fully trained nurse, she was pregnant in Manchester before she could find a job. Mike didn't seem to know what he was doing – forever dreaming up new schemes, talking of computers and other crazy ideas he knew little about. So yes, that made her hard too. But she also changed politically; viewing the North from a distance was not like having to live there. The indifference in Britain, the ignorance of what was happening in a part of what they called the United Kingdom. That stupid, heartless fucking bitch Thatcher – Margaret hated sharing her name, and watched as Thatcher moved on from one confrontation to the next. The miners must have been easy after standing by to watch ten men die on hunger strike – but then they were only miners, they were only common criminals. Margaret saw a lot of things on television and heard a lot of things on the radio – you do when you're stuck in the house with a young baby and another on the way.

Mike pulled through with the help of his friend Eugene from college. He was right about computers after all, and he and Eugene went into business together as training consultants. There were a lot of companies out there, keen to implement the new technology but without a clue as to how to go about it. Mike understood very little of what actually went on inside a computer – he had Eugene for that – but his ignorance helped him win over customers. He was also very good at seeing potential uses for the innovations Eugene enthused about; Eugene thought something was wonderful in itself, while Mike thought something was wonderful because of what it could do. They were the saving of each other – Mike made enough money to support his family, and Eugene enjoyed playing the boffin to Mike's salesman.

Margaret knew that Mike kept at least an eye on the financial markets and that he earned a certain amount from the investments he'd made, but she was surprised that he didn't make more. Mike missed for example the large amounts of money to be made on IBM and Apple, despite having Eugene as an ear to the ground when it came to computing. When the stock values crashed in these companies, it was strange to Margaret that Mike hadn't made a fortune and got out in time – that would have been the Mike of old. When she asked him about it, he just said you had to be at it full time to stay ahead of the markets. Besides, everybody was into the stock market now that Thatcher was offering shares in every nationalized industry she could sell off.

Mike did accurately predict when Thatcher would go.

'The men in grey suits have had enough of her,' he said.

Margaret couldn't understand how they could just get rid of Thatcher – couldn't picture life without her, actually.

'She is still the prime minister,' she said. 'She won't let go that easily.'

'You just watch,' said Mike. 'She's only had the power because they allowed her the power, and now she's become a liability.'

Mike was so confident of his prediction that he broke a promise to himself and placed a bet on Thatcher being gone by a certain date. He didn't win that much money, but he enjoyed being right. One of Margaret's happiest memories was of the three of them – herself, Mike and Eugene – quietly cracking open a bottle of champagne to celebrate Thatcher's defeat. The children were upstairs in bed and Margaret had told Mike that evening that she was going to return to work within the next year. She felt good about her decision and it was somehow tied in to the fact that Thatcher was finally gone. She stood huddled with Mike and Eugene in the corner of the living room. Mike had rolled a joint and they passed it one to the other, three friends together, smoking and drinking the champagne. Eugene had set up a video loop of Thatcher's tears, and it was playing over and over on the television screen. He had told them he had a girlfriend he was seeing – Eugene! Even though they had the whole of the room to themselves, it seemed important to be so close and that they should have their arms around each other. Margaret kissed first Mike and then Eugene.

That was a good day.

So, would Mike leave her? Margaret thought not, on the whole.

In the past year or so Margaret had noticed a change in Mike, and she knew he'd decided to try again. Of the two of them, it was Mike who was trying the harder to move on and to get over what had happened. She watched as he eventually got a hold on his early anger and rage, and suspected this was his reason for working away from Manchester more frequently than in the past – to avoid her, and to avoid going off on another rant. They both hated losing control, especially when the children were around to pick up a vibe, and when it hit Mike, it hit him hard. Margaret knew that absenting himself from the family home was just about Mike's only defence mechanism

She told Mike once that she'd never have done it if she'd known he'd take it so badly.

'How the fuck did you think I would take it?' asked Mike. 'That I would understand?'

'I didn't think you were that bothered,' said Margaret.

Of course, Mike's screaming years didn't do much to help Margaret's guilt, and now he'd changed it seemed too late. She listened as he told her that the only solution he could see was to simply love her again. He was sorry for everything that had happened, and he was sorry if it was because of something he had done – or hadn't done. He hoped things never got that bad between them again.

But in the five years since Margaret had been unfaithful – five years, half a decade, gone by just like that – she still couldn't forgive herself. She just felt so guilty, all the time, all day, every day, every place she went and everything she tried to do. She just felt sick when Mike came on to her. They'd be getting along fine, things almost like normal – whatever that might be – and Mike would go to put his arms around her or kiss her on the lips, and Margaret would just freeze and the moment would be lost. And then Mike would be angry again, and a few more months would go by. If Margaret couldn't get over what she'd done, there was little hope that Mike could do it alone. They had to move on together; if not, then perhaps Mike would have to leave after all.

Margaret dreaded Mike talking to her about it, dreaded being on her own with him because it was all he ever talked about, and so she gradually just shut herself down. She hated being this way and she could see what she was doing was making Mike pay, in a way, all over again, for something she had done in the first place. She knew what he was saying – loving each other was the only way out of this mess – but she couldn't give herself to him in that way anymore. She might in the future – she didn't know – but right now she hated herself too much, hated her body too much and hated the thought of intimacy more than anything. Or perhaps it was just her age and a physical thing she was going through?

Whichever, this was why she was lying alone in her bed. Not that they slept together at all these days – again, Margaret couldn't. They'd tried to continue sharing their bed but sometimes Mike got so agitated in the night that he prevented them both from sleeping. It made sense on nights like this for Mike to move into Jack's vacated room. Then, one time when Mike returned from being away, he didn't even try to share the bed with Margaret and had slept on his own ever since. At least this way they could both sleep through the night. God knows what the kids thought. Margaret had watched her own parents grow apart and yet maintain a workable understanding in front of the children – she'd sworn never to be like her mother but here she was, more like her than ever. It was even stranger now Mike and she were the only ones in the house, but even this wasn't enough of a prompt for them to sleep together. Margaret couldn't see how they could ever be close like that again – even if she got over what was happening to her, there was too much history to ever go back to the way things were.

Mike's simple solution of just loving each other again irritated the hell out of her.

'I don't know why you think we can just go back to how we were twenty years ago,' she said.

She knew Mike didn't mean that, but he didn't bother to argue the point. She guessed that by now he just accepted it . . . if she didn't want him, she didn't want him.

And Margaret, she could either lie in bed going over and over the same old shit or she could get on with her day, and this was what she chose to do. She had been surprised when Mike said he was going to Dublin for the day but she didn't think it was another defensive manoeuvre; she guessed he had business there after all. Now that she was awake, with little chance of getting back to sleep, she planned the day.

She wasn't working today – she operated a three-day job-share at Withington Hospital – but she had more than enough things to do. She was coming to the end of a professional course in counselling and for the past few months she'd been holding sessions with a handful of clients each week. She had two booked for today, one at eleven and one at two. These were part of her coursework and had to be written up in full afterwards. She also had some project work to complete and hoped to get this done first thing before she went out for the day. She volunteered at the Rape Crisis Centre when she wasn't working or at college, mostly afternoons and evenings but with the occasional night shift every few weeks. If Mike wasn't going to be back until quite late, Margaret could extend her afternoon shift at the centre and possibly complete her project work there.

The counselling course had finally given Margaret the sense of self-esteem she'd been missing as a nurse. Whatever Mike said about nursing, however hard he'd tried to make her see the worth of what she was doing, Margaret had never valued it as she would, say, a law degree. She'd gone straight into nursing from school, and had always felt in awe of Mike's education.

'But that's because you've never been to university,' said Mike. 'You learn more on the ward in one week than I did in a whole term of college – and it's a lot more use, believe me.'

'So why do they have degree courses in nursing then?'

'I don't know,' said Mike. 'You've said yourself that college nurses have to relearn everything they think they know. And besides, you've actually passed all those same exams – you just didn't go to college to do it.'

There was no telling Margaret. It wasn't exactly an inferiority thing, because she knew she was a better nurse than any college graduate; it was more a respect for something that she'd never experienced herself. It was very easy for Mike to talk about the idiots and fools he met in college; he was there – studying for a law degree, no less. No amount of talk about drink and drugs and easy-to-pass exams could convince Margaret otherwise. Just as when Mike first came back to Belfast on vacation from college in Manchester, nothing he could say would convince her they'd ever be together. Margaret was in Belfast and Mike was in Manchester; she was from the Falls and he might as well have been from another planet.

But the counselling course was different; it was a natural progression from nursing and something Margaret could call her own. Her days on the course, away from the job-share at the hospital, really felt like going to college; the exams and coursework were certainly real enough and she was good at it, she knew. Perhaps she'd just needed to be at a certain age to be ready for this? She couldn't imagine her younger self having the confidence to embark on a new career.

It wasn't entirely how Margaret had imagined it – a lot of the newer theory was directed towards the patient working things through alone. As a counsellor, Margaret had to accompany the patient, rather than lead them down the path to recovery. But even if it wasn't always quite what she'd expected, Margaret was proud of her studies; she liked the discipline of applying what she'd learnt and was going to stick at it.

She pushed back the covers and stepped down from the bed. It was seven thirty-seven. She went through to the bathroom to take her shower.

Margaret had taken to shaving herself between her legs every day. For years she'd had an ambivalent attitude to shaving under her arms – she liked it when she did and she liked it when she didn't. Mike said it was very European not to shave under her arms and seemed not to mind – seemed to quite like it in fact. She did her legs every few days and had only never bothered when she was feeling particularly down, when the kids were growing up and it didn't seem to matter one way or the other. It had been a part of her coming out of a depression, a part of feeling better about herself, and making the effort for her own sake as much as for Mike's, but these days it was an integral part of her shower. She started shaving between her legs about a year ago after reading how healthy and clean it was meant to be. She continued because she liked how it felt – it felt clean but it also felt a little sexy; a little bit of wild that only Margaret knew about. She knew Mike would like it but they were a long way from that – this had to be for herself.

One of the joys of being alone in the house was walking naked with her towel from the bathroom back to her bedroom; the house was too old to have an en suite built in and they liked the bedroom too much to change it. Margaret picked out her underwear. The older she'd become, the more expensive was her under-wear; again, it would have been nice to share how good she looked, but these days she made do with how good she felt. She tended to dress up for her counselling sessions, or dress smartly at least. She had a long skirt that she favoured, and a silk blouse and a suit jacket. Margaret's clothes were an essential part of her preparation for the day. She checked herself in the mirror and, satisfied with how she looked, she took off her jacket and replaced it with an old sweatshirt. She still had a couple of hours' project work to do before she left the house. She returned the towel to the bathroom and carried her jacket downstairs.

Margaret made herself a full pot of coffee. She alternated using a plunger jug with an espresso pot heated on the stove, depending on the type of coffee she'd opened; today it was filter coffee in the plunger. She boiled the water in the kettle and then poured in a small amount to warm the jug. She swirled the water around the upper part of the jug, trying to heat each part of the glass, and then emptied the water into the sink. She took the jar of coffee from the fridge and filled out four heaped scoops into the jug. She replaced the top on the coffee jar and returned it to the fridge. Without reboiling the kettle, she poured in enough water to cover the coffee and waited to let it seep into the grounds. She shook the jug to make sure the water permeated through to all the coffee. Every time she did this she thought of the movie *Betty Blue*, the scene where they're making the coffee and waiting in awkward silence while they let the coffee grounds soak in the pan. Margaret poured in the rest of the boiled water to the top of the jug. She placed the plunger in the jug and rested it on top of the coffee. She took a tea towel from the rack on the front of the stove and wrapped it around the coffee jug.

While she was waiting for the coffee, Margaret cleared the kitchen table and wiped it down with a cloth. She kept her college bag on the shoe rack behind the kitchen door; she took out the books for her project and set them out across the kitchen table. She left a space to her right for her coffee and toast.

She took a mug from the cupboard and poured in some of the water that was still in the kettle; she did the same with a plate. She hated using cold crockery and she liked her toast to stay warm once it was ready to eat. She took two slices of bread from the packet in the bread bin, put them in the toaster, and pushed down the lever. She tipped the hot water from the mug into the sink and reached up to the cupboard for the sugar. Using the teaspoon in the sugar bowl, she put a single spoonful into the mug. She left the spoon in the mug and returned the bowl to the cupboard. She unwrapped the towel from the coffee jug, plunged down the plunger and poured the coffee into the mug. She stirred the sugar into the coffee. She tipped the hot water from the plate into the sink and dried the plate with the towel. When the toast popped up, she placed it on the plate and reached for a jar of honey that was kept by the side of the kettle. Using the spoon from her coffee, she scooped some honey on to each piece of toast and then threw the spoon into the sink. She carried her coffee and toast over to the kitchen table and sat down.

Margaret drank her coffee and ate her toast as she read over the work she already had done on her project.

It was ironic, Margaret thought, that she was now the only member of her family to show the slightest interest in going to college. Her children certainly weren't bothered; they seemed to have picked up on their father's low opinion of what studying for a degree might bring them. Jack had tried college for a while, if only for his mother's sake; but he couldn't stick it and seemed happier now he'd come out and told her. Mike junior didn't even bother to pretend.

'What would I want to do that for?' he asked. He wanted to see places and earn money.

Margaret was disappointed, but disappointed in the way of all parents who have never been to college and want the best for their children.

She cleared away her plate and washed the crumbs of toast and sticky honey from her hands. She washed the teaspoon at the same time and, without drying the spoon, took down the sugar bowl again from the cupboard and poured herself some more coffee. She settled down to work and studied like this for almost an hour before being disturbed by the front-door bell.

Margaret was tempted to ignore it — the kitchen was a long way back, through the hallway, from the front of the house, and she couldn't be seen from the front door. But when the bell rang a second time, she decided to answer the door and take it as a sign that she'd done enough work for now. She looked at the time – it was almost ten o'clock – and she knew she should be getting ready to leave.

Margaret walked along the hallway and saw through the glass in the front door that it was Eugene. She wasn't surprised, but she regretted not anticipating who it might be; it was too late now though.

'Eugene,' she said.

'Margaret,' he said. 'May I come in?'

She opened the door wide and stood to one side.

'You can,' said Margaret, 'but I'm on my way out.'

Eugene hesitated; he smiled a lopsided smile, and then looked back down to the ground.

'I'm through in the kitchen,' said Margaret, and walked back into the house.

Eugene didn't follow her, and Margaret took the opportunity to grab the things she needed for the morning. She pulled off her sweatshirt and picked up her jacket. She took a second to make sure she hadn't forgotten anything. She had thought she might take everything with her for the day, but now she'd have to come back for the afternoon's case file. She picked up her bag and checked for her car keys inside.

'I was looking for Mike,' said Eugene down the hallway.

'Well, he's not here,' said Margaret. She pushed past Eugene and pulled the door to behind her. Eugene had to step back from the porch of the house.

'Margaret – '

'I'm late, Eugene,' said Margaret. 'I told you – Mike's not here.'

'I know, but I – '

'So why come looking for him then?'

'Because it's actually you that I really want to speak to,' said Eugene.

Margaret locked the front door.

'Well, it'll have to wait,' she said. 'I have a counselling session at eleven, and it's out at Alderley Edge.'

Margaret walked down the steps in front of the house.

'Please, Margaret – '

'I told you,' she said again. 'I'm late.'

Margaret walked through the gate and into the street. She pressed the remote for her Renault Clio, got in and drove away.

2

Katie's meeting went on for an hour. It was her meeting, so there was nowhere to hide, and she had to put Mike's phone call to the back of her mind. She was relieved Carmel wasn't in the room.

This was Katie's weekly get-together with her three trainees, to go over the changes and fluctuations in the accounts they'd been given. She could have gone over them individually, but this way one person's mistake was everybody's lesson. She knew of course what was happening to the accounts before the meeting but she let the trainees describe what was going on. She encouraged them to be open about what they were doing – they might as well be if she already knew – and there were never any recriminations at this stage of their training. Nobody actually changed the make-up of a portfolio without first going through Katie. She tried to have the trainees focus separately on currencies, stocks and bonds so they each brought something different to the table.

Katie wasn't herself but she got through the hour. When she returned to her office, though, it was impossible to avoid Carmel's look of concern.

'Are you okay?' asked Carmel.

'Fine, thanks,' said Katie, but she didn't linger by

Carmel's desk to pick up her messages. And she closed her door, something Katie only ever did if she was in a meeting or on a very difficult call.

What the hell was Mike thinking? Because he was in trouble, he was determined to drag Katie down as well? So much for all his grand gestures when he set up the scam, keeping Katie well away from the stock purchase of Halibro. Unless they'd followed where the money went next? But if she didn't actually do anything, could they chase her for the money – or prosecute her for fraud? Would they really pursue it so far? And could they really touch Katie in a different jurisdiction? The movement of money was international but, unlike Mike, she wasn't an American citizen; they knew where they could stick their subpoena if they tried it on her.

What was the most likely thing to happen? That they would try to stop her trading? That was easily done. Just a hint of an association with what Mike had pulled off was enough to say goodbye to her job. Let's face it, they could do whatever they liked if they put their minds to it.

Is this what Mike was contacting her to warn her about? Well, she'd been ready for twenty years to walk at a moment's notice. Her money was safe and her passport was in her bag. Mike was more exposed, it was true, but there was little Katie could do to help him. She didn't believe for one minute that he was scared, and even if he was – what was it to her?

If they followed the money to her then they could follow it elsewhere – to Bruno, for instance.

So Mike knew how to find her – how like Mike. Katie could have tracked Mike down too, if she'd chosen to, but she hadn't. Did he come across her by chance – this was likely, given her high profile over these past few years – or had he sought her out? Was he watching her before they found him? This was Mike, remember; of course he was watching her – watching but not contacting, as agreed. Perhaps, unlike Katie, Mike didn't need the clean break to see it through? Was he watching out of concern, to see that she was okay? Well, she'd been okay for a long while now – at least by the measure of the world – so what was he playing at?

Come on, Katie; stop fucking around! You know exactly what's going on here. Stop pretending – this is about Bruno and you know it.

There was a knock at Katie's door and Carmel walked in. She closed the door behind her and sat down in the chair by Katie's desk.

'Carmel?'

It was obvious to Katie that Carmel didn't really know how to put whatever it was she'd decided to say.

'Carmel,' said Katie, 'if this is about this morning and my being rude, I'm sorry. It won't happen again.'

'No,' said Carmel, 'it's not about that; at least, not about you being rude. You're the boss and bosses are rude sometimes – '

'That's no – '

'But you aren't, usually, so don't worry. God knows you're a weird fuck, but one thing you're not generally is rude.'

Katie smiled.

'So,' she said, 'apart from telling me I'm a weird fuck – what is it?'

'That phone call, this morning – '

'I don't want to talk about it,' said Katie. 'He won't be calling again, that's all.'

'But it's not all, is it?' asked Carmel. 'As I said, you're a weird fuck and you keep yourself to yourself and that's fine, especially in your position. I know I gossip and everything but it doesn't mean anything and that's not why I'm here – to find out what's going on. So, I don't know what that was all about this morning and I don't want to know – well, I do want to know but I know I'm not going to find out, so I might as well pretend I don't care – but I do care about you and I can see you're upset, so that's why I came in.'

Katie nodded that she understood. 'I appreciate it, Carmel, I do, but there's nothing to be done about it and I'll be fine.'

'I don't think so,' said Carmel.

'What do you mean – if I say I'll be fine then I'll be fine, surely?'

'Not necessarily; in fact, no, I don't think so. Tell me to mind my own business if you like; as I said, you're the boss – '

'Stop saying that,' said Katie.

'Well you are,' said Carmel, 'but the one thing you never do is insult my intelligence, so don't start now. If you've had a shock or an upset, or if this person is bothering you, then it's okay to ask for my help. Or take the rest of the day off to get it sorted, that's all I'm saying. Everybody has shit going on in their lives; it's bound to surface sooner or later, and you don't necessarily want to be in work when it does. Do you hear what I'm saying?'

'I do,' said Katie. 'I do.'

'After all, you are – '

'The boss; yes, I know. Thanks, Carmel; really, thanks.'

'Just don't . . . well, just don't whatever, okay?'

'I won't,' said Katie. 'I promise.'

But as Carmel left the room, Katie still didn't know what she would do about Mike. She knew it was pointless to stay in work – Carmel was at least right about that. There was nothing that couldn't be left to another day. Katie's attendance record was more or less perfect. Better to think this through at home than behind the closed door of her office.

But even then, she thought, nothing would be resolved without seeing Mike.

Damn him and damn whatever he was about.

Okay. Think; breathe.

Mike would know that Bruno had never collected the money. Mike would know everything because he always did. Stop! There's no way he could know about Bruno, so is that what he's here to find out? Because if they're looking for the money, they'll be looking for Bruno, and Mike doesn't know where that might lead? And he wants to make sure it leads to Katie and not to Mike?

Fucking hell, Katie – come on; think this through. Nobody knows about Bruno. It was twenty years ago. If he was ever found, he couldn't have been recognized. If he had been recognized they would have traced him to Katie and not to Mike. She was the one travelling with Bruno. She was the one sharing a room. They may have paid cash, but the hotel had Katie's correct name from her passport. The airline had her travelling alone next to Bruno's empty seat. Despite what she had thought at the time, it was so traceable a connection, it would have taken only days – hours even – to find Katie. This case was closed; except maybe not now if they were looking for the money?

They had Mike; without Mike, would they find Katie? Did they know where the money had gone? Surely Mike was clever enough to move the money around to cover his tracks? Or was there a direct link between Mike and Bruno's money? Take away Mike and what did they have on Katie?

What did she mean – take away Mike? Killing Bruno was one thing; even that she'd messed up, big time. Why did she take that stupid model of the MGM Grand back from the car to Bruno? It was like saying – here, you probably can't recognize this person, but I've left you this clue to let you know where he was staying. Oh, and by the way, that's what I used to kill him!

Fucking idiot! Why? Bruno was still alive at the time; Katie thought he was dead, but he was still alive. He might have died out there in the desert, but there was nothing on Bruno – no passport, no tickets – so why did Katie go back to him? It didn't make any sense, unless it was to make sure – unless she had wanted to kill him.

Katie felt absolutely no remorse at killing Bruno; what she regretted was losing the run of herself at the time. It was like a maths equation – Bruno did this thing so Katie had to kill him – a simple equation with absolute logic. She knew she would do the same again; but if it was so straightforward, why did Katie mess it up at the time? She obviously wasn't very good at it and here she was, thinking of doing it again.

Was her life that good? Was Katie so happy with the life she had that she'd do anything to keep it?

She wasn't going to kill Mike. She'd only killed . . . she'd only killed Bruno because of what he tried to do.

Maybe it wasn't her fault? Maybe what happened wasn't her fault?

Katie checked in her bag for her passport. If she had to run away again then so be it, but she couldn't just keep running away.

It made sense to see Mike first, to see what he knew. But was she strong enough? And did it leave her exposed?

Katie stood up; she'd made her decision. She had to find out why Mike was in Dublin. Once she'd done that, she could decide what to do next.

She picked up her coat and bag and walked out of her office. She told Carmel she was leaving for the day; she could see that Carmel approved.

*

Leaving the Financial Services Centre during the day was like stepping from one world into another. Behind Katie were the banks and the offices and, further back, the enclosed apartments of the reclaimed docks – all very nice. To her left was the Customs House, isolated in its grandeur by the traffic that converged from several directions at once. The trucks still arrived from Dublin Port on the north bank of the river, looking to cross over to the south side and then on through town before heading west. They preferred to pay the charge for travelling through the city than take the tunnel in the wrong direction and queue to pay a toll. Traffic from Amiens Street waited to cross the river; traffic from Gardiner Street waited to cross the river; traffic from the north quays did a loop-the-loop around the Customs House, and waited to cross the river. You couldn't have dreamt it up; such a crazy scheme could only have evolved over many years, and nobody ever seemed to ask why.

In front of Katie was Busáras, the award-winning building that housed the bus station – only the SIPTU building was as ugly. She crossed over the road and cut behind the station onto Gardiner Street. The street was dominated by bed and breakfast businesses that sold themselves on being so close to the city centre. If you checked their location on a map, you would see they were right but you wouldn't see why they were so cheap. This was where a lot of visitors to Dublin stayed, and this was where a lot of visitors to Dublin were mugged; it was what they called a tourist industry. Up Gardiner

Street to the right and you were in Summerhill; up to the left and you were on Parnell Street – one of the nastiest places Katie had seen in the world, let alone in Dublin.

She crossed over the road and walked up Talbot Street towards O'Connell Street. Loudspeakers announced the bargains to be had inside the shops, proud of their tackiness and sure of their market. Piles of refuse sacks stood outside the fast-food joints; a guy walked past pulling an open cart of collected rubbish, but he didn't do the sacks – that was someone else's job. Another guy with a huge vacuum cleaner thing made his way along Talbot Street in the opposite direction, but still the street was filthy. The path was splattered with dis-carded chewing gum – how long before the dirty white stuff, spat from people's mouths, was allowed to cover the whole pavement?

Katie turned into O'Connell Street.

This city is a shit hole, she thought.

What was wrong with her? This wasn't why Katie had come to live in Ireland. She used to love this country.

Katie stepped into the Gresham Hotel; here at least was some escape from the toilet that was Dublin. She crossed over to the reception desk, but saw Mike towards the back of the foyer, sat in an armchair reading the paper. He still looked like Mike, a little fuller per-haps but with the same fresh, young man's face. She always associated Mike's face with the Antrim coast above Belfast – not that she'd ever been there, but still that was how she thought of him.

As Katie walked across towards Mike, she could see he was lost in thought and not in the newspaper; but then, knowing Mike, he could have seen Katie and was putting on an act.

'Hey, Maguire,' she said.

Mike looked up and smiled. The greeting was the same one he'd called over to Katie when he'd first seen her walking along Oxford Road, on her way to the library in the middle of the night.

'Hey, McGuire,' he said. 'How are you?' Mike stood up from the armchair and they hugged.

Katie was surprised by how much Mike put into the hug; she was a little ashamed that she didn't feel the same rush of emotion.

'Thanks for coming,' said Mike. 'I appreciate it, really, I do.'

'You gave me little choice,' said Katie, and sat down.

'Can I get you anything – a drink, or a sandwich maybe?'

'I'm fine for now, thanks,' she said. Katie was determined not to stay or, rather, to stay only as long as she needed to. She was uncomfortable with this and said as much to Mike.

'We had a deal,' she said, 'and you broke it.'

Mike looked down at the ground.

Still so young, thought Katie.

She might have had only a couple of years on Mike, but there was something refreshingly naive about how easy he was to read – a terrible face for a card player, when you got right down to it.

'You'll see why,' he said, 'when I tell you. And I'm not putting you in any danger by being here. Gosh, it's good to see you.'

'Gosh?' asked Katie.

'Yes, gosh,' said Mike, and smiled. 'You look well, very well in fact.'

'Thank you,' said Katie. She decided it was pointless to rush this. She realized her emotions were all over the place – what else would explain that agitated walk from the office? She needed to gather herself here.

Katie called over to a passing waiter.

'I will have a drink, after all,' she said to Mike. 'I'll have a vodka and orange,' she ordered, 'and . . . ?'

'Just an orange juice, no vodka,' said Mike.

'Are you driving?' she asked, once the waiter had left them.

'No, just a long day ahead, and yes, I suppose, when I get back to Manchester I have to drive home from the airport.'

'You moved back to Manchester, then?' asked Katie.

'Yes,' said Mike. 'More or less immediately after college. I was never going to settle in Belfast, so a few months after Vegas I decided Manchester was . . .'

'The place for you?'

'The place I felt most comfortable with.'

The mention of Vegas came too soon – neither Katie nor Mike was ready to talk about why they were here just yet.

'What about you?' asked Mike. 'When did you move

to Ireland? I thought you had that job lined up in London?'

Katie suspected that Mike knew exactly where she'd been for the past twenty years; she was tempted to say as much to him, but she let it go.

'Yes,' she said, 'I took that job in London. I actually delayed starting work for a few months so I could travel a bit – make up for lost time, maybe.'

'So where did you go?' asked Mike.

'Oh, mainly around Europe at first, throughout that summer after college, but then further afield once I'd started work. It came to be my thing – you know, extended holidays to far-off places. I used to take the bulk of my holiday allowance in one go; it was all I needed it for anyway.'

'So,' asked Mike again, 'where did you go?'

'Oh, India, Africa, Australia, Asia; some places were nicer than others.'

'And do you still travel to the same extent?'

'No,' said Katie, 'I've kind of stopped ever since moving to Ireland. Living here seemed to soothe the travel itch. But I've been thinking about South America recently; it feels like I might be picking up the bug again. I'd want to do it properly though, learn the languages and everything, and stay for long enough to make it worth my while.'

'And when did you move to Ireland?' asked Mike.

'At the end of the eighties. I'd really done the London thing and I liked the sound of what they were trying to do here – you know, setting up the

Financial Services Centre, kick-starting the economy again, that sort of thing. It was either here or New York and . . .'

And she wasn't going to set foot in North America again, was what she'd thought at the time. She let it go now without saying as much to Mike.

'I'd changed companies a few times by then,' said Katie, 'and I was offered the chance to set up an office here.'

'It sounds as though you've done well,' said Mike.

'We all made a lot of money, if that's what you mean. But I was ready for a change; I was sick of England and everything it had become.'

'They were pretty nasty times,' said Mike.

'Nasty times, yes,' said Katie. 'Fairly clear-cut times, as well; it seemed you were either on one side or the other, and I didn't really like the side I was on.'

'What do you mean?'

'Well, at the time of the poll tax riots, for example, I was living in London watching this pitched battle on TV. It was just a few miles away, but for all the world seemed like it was on another planet.'

'You mean you had money and they didn't?'

'No,' said Katie, 'it wasn't just that. It was . . . well it wasn't a riot for a start. It wasn't even a pitched battle. It was mounted police charging and batoning crowds of people – unarmed people, disenfranchised people if they didn't pay the tax – and I didn't like it. So, as I say, fairly clear-cut times.'

'It wasn't pleasant,' agreed Mike.

'I didn't feel as though I belonged to either side,' said Katie. 'Certainly not with the police and the government. I just didn't like the way things were going.'

'So you got out?'

'Something like that; only now I don't know whether it was England I was fed up with or London. I do know I was glad to leave when I did.'

'And there was me thinking Maggie's Britain would suit you just fine.'

'The money suited me,' said Katie, 'but I didn't like what it was doing to society.'

'There's no such thing as society, remember?'

'Who could forget?'

'And will you stay in Ireland?' asked Mike.

'Who knows?' said Katie. 'Where's he gone with our drinks, do you think? I'm ready for my vodka now.'

'He's probably still trying to open the carton of orange juice,' said Mike. 'Have you seen those new openers – where you have to twist off the top and it rips your hand to pieces?'

Katie laughed.

'I mean, how difficult can it be?' asked Mike.

'To design an opener that actually works?' said Katie. 'And pours out the juice without spilling and dripping, everywhere but into the glass? Come off it, Mike – you ask for too much.'

'Maybe he's squeezing fresh oranges for us?' suggested Mike.

'Right,' said Katie. 'This is Dublin, remember?'

'Here he is now.'

The waiter placed down the drinks and handed Mike the receipt. Mike paid for the drinks.

'I thought of you,' he said to Katie, 'when I was paying the taxi fare into town. The driver was friendly enough – no racism – and I thought maybe you'd been exaggerating in your articles.'

'And then?'

'Well, the fare was over nineteen euros, which I thought was a bit steep, to tell you the truth. I gave your man a twenty and he started taking an age to find the change, obviously waiting for me to say forget it, twenty's fine. But I didn't think twenty was fine, so I waited to see how long he'd play the change game, and it went on until he became so pissed he just gave me the money. No more friendly taxi driver – he drove off without a word of goodbye before I'd even shut the door.'

'Welcome to Dublin,' said Katie.

They clinked glasses.

'I enjoy reading your pieces in the paper,' said Mike.

'Hmm,' said Katie. 'I think it's got a little out of hand.'

'What do you mean?' asked Mike.

'I enjoyed it at first,' said Katie, 'and, you know, it made me feel important, but now I'm not so sure.'

'What do you mean?' asked Mike again.

'Well, the early stuff was very much aimed at the government and how it's running the economy. Like, I've lived through Thatcherism once; I don't need to live through it again.'

'But Ireland's done well, surely?'

'From a distance, maybe – just like the eighties were great in Britain if you didn't have to live there.'

'But is it really Thatcherism that's happening here?' asked Mike.

'No,' said Katie, 'they don't even have the balls for that. At least you knew where you were with Maggie: she'd send in the troops to get what she wanted, or seize your funds in the courts, or whatever.'

'And here?'

'Here they're still stuck into gombeen politics. They talk of things like zero tolerance, but then they don't enforce it.'

'Would you want them to?'

'No,' said Katie, 'but anything would be better than these incompetents; all they're good at is looking after their own and staying in power.'

'So,' said Mike, 'maybe that's why your editor keeps asking you to write for the paper?'

'I'm tired, Mike,' said Katie, 'really tired. I feel like all I do now is bellyache about the shit things I see. They've got used to me and put me in a box and, sure, they let me have my say, but I'm becoming a caricature of myself.'

'I think you're better than that,' said Mike.

'Have you read that Nick Hornby book, *How to be Good*?'

'I've seen it, but not read it,' said Mike.

'Yes, well, there's a character in it – he writes a news-paper column and calls himself the Angriest Man in

Holloway. I feel like that: once I start off on my rant, I can't seem to get off it.'

'But you obviously do it well.'

'I know,' said Katie, 'but I think it's time to call it a day. It's all people have come to expect off me, and their reaction always comes back to the fact that I'm English. No matter what I talk about, it's my Englishness – or my non-Irishness – that they're interested in, and not the issues.'

'But it's very entertaining,' said Mike, and smiled.

'It doesn't get anything changed, though. Jesus, they'll talk about something for years and not feel the need to do anything about it.'

'Ah, there, now you are sounding English. You can't expect people to just go ahead and do things, to actually achieve or change anything.'

'But I'm sick of all that modern-life-is-rubbish stuff,' said Katie. 'I mean, it is rubbish but once you start noticing things it becomes a compulsion – it's impossible to stop. You walk into a public lavatory and there's no room to stand to close the door. The toilet roll dispenser that can't dispense the toilet roll; the washbasin tap that soaks the front of your dress; the hand dryer that doesn't dry your hands – they're all clichés of modern life, but that doesn't stop them being repeated over and over again. Why would someone go to the trouble of manufacturing a hand dryer that doesn't actually dry hands?'

'You see,' said Mike. 'You're good at it.'

'But it's all so shit,' said Katie, 'and I can't stop

thinking about it. It's like there's not enough in my life that I can ignore the shit I see all around me.'

'Time for a change, then?'

'I guess so,' said Katie, 'but I don't know what.'

'The world is full of crappy things, it's true, but if you think too much about them it'll drive you crazy. And don't think for one moment that things are any different in England, because they're not.'

'Oh I know all about England,' said Katie, 'with its tunnel-vision barmen who can only cope with one customer at a time, and the lottery of who they might choose to serve next – waiting for that special moment when they turn from the till and you hope to God you catch their eye. And calling time exactly on eleven, with ten minutes' drinking-up time – they're so fucking anal. I'm not sure I could stand all that again. Maybe I just need a holiday, or a break at least – South America might be a little drastic.'

'You could come and visit us in Manchester,' said Mike.

'I don't think so,' said Katie.

Katie was aware that she'd reduced her life to such an extent that it was bound to result in a narrowing of her stimuli. You can only pick up a certain amount through the reading of a newspaper. She wasn't exactly hiding in Ireland, but it was easier to control how she encountered the outside world. Her colleagues thought her excessively private; her position didn't exactly encourage familiarity, and a lot of them were happy not to be chummy with the boss. Of course, her sexuality was a constant source of fascination, but this was preferable to them knowing every gory detail of her private life. But Katie knew that, really, this was no way to live her life.

She also knew that, without even trying, Mike had got more information out of her than she was comfortable with.

'What about you, Mike?' she asked. 'Did you stay in banking or not?'

'There were three business types,' said Mike, by way of an answer, 'sat over there on the next table, an hour or so before you arrived. You know, suits and talking too loud and laughing. And I thought, is that really what I look like when I'm doing my stuff?'

'Only you don't notice so much when it's you?'

'Yeah, something like that – all three of them talking and not one of them listening to what the others were saying. One guy was the know-it-all – '

'That'd be you, then?'

'Very funny. One was the know-it-all and you could tell the other two couldn't stand him – '

'Definitely you,' said Katie.

'But then they couldn't stand each other either. They all thought they were the one – the one most likely – and it was all about refrigeration, or some such shit.'

'Or banking – is that what you mean?' asked Katie. 'It's all shit, Mike; I thought you knew that better than all of us?'

Mike continued. 'The know-it-all – the big man – he didn't wash his hands after using the toilet.'

'He what?' asked Katie.

'He used the toilet and didn't wash his hands – I saw him.'

'You followed him to the toilet?'

'I didn't follow him,' said Mike. 'We happened to be there at the same time.'

'And he didn't wash his hands – are you sure?'

'Most men don't bother to wash their hands.'

'Some maybe, but not most?' asked Katie.

'Believe me,' said Mike; 'most men don't wash their hands after using the toilet. You notice your things and put them in your newspaper – well, I notice my things and that's one of the things I've noticed.'

'That's gross,' said Katie.

'At least two out of every three, I'd say. So two out of those three business types – two out of the three refrigerator men – go straight from the toilet and back into the bar for their drink.'

'I'm not sure I'd want them to be looking in my refrigerator, not with habits like that,' said Katie.

'Think about that the next time some bloke is chatting you up and offers to buy you a drink.'

Katie smiled. They sat quietly for a moment or two.

'So, Mike,' she said, 'are you going to tell me what you've done for the past twenty years, or do I have to beat it out of you? Did your early banking fraud ever catch up with you?'

'You mean all those accounts I used to run when I first went to college? No, they must have been on too small a scale for them to care; I guess they were written off in the end. I bet you've written off millions in your time, haven't you?'

'The larger the amount,' said Katie, 'the easier it is to write off. But the little guys, we normally stick to them like shit. I'd have hounded you into the ground if it was my bank's money.'

'Some of it probably was,' said Mike. 'I don't think there was a bank in Manchester that I didn't open some form of an account in.'

'What did you do after college then?' asked Katie. 'Did you ever follow up on your scholarship?'

'No,' said Mike. 'I'd had enough of banking and investments for one lifetime. I didn't really do much for a while – I went back to Belfast, but I couldn't stick that for much longer than a summer. Even when I moved over to Manchester again, I wasn't really sure what I was going to do.'

Mike hesitated for a moment.

'I was getting over you, actually,' he said. 'I knew where you were working, or where I guessed you were working, and I was very tempted to try to find you.'

'What were you using for money?'

'I had a bit of money but not that much and I knew I couldn't go on like that forever. I just couldn't seem to get going again; anything I thought of doing never really amounted to much. You know, I was even beginning to doubt myself.'

'No,' said Katie, and smiled, 'not the great Mike Maguire?'

'It's true, it's true,' said Mike. 'It was a new experience

for me and I didn't like it, not one bit. Every week there'd be more factories closing, industries being shut down and another million on the dole. I was beginning to think I didn't have the luxury of turning down jobs from investment bankers who had paid my way through college.'

Of course Mike didn't mention that he might well have been prosecuted if he'd tried to work for an investment bank, but Katie let this pass.

'So what happened?' she asked. 'What did you do in the end?'

'It was Eugene, actually,' said Mike, 'who helped me out eventually. Do you remember Eugene, from college?'

'Of course I do,' said Katie. There were so few people who had actually featured in Katie's life, it wasn't hard to remember them all.

'Well, we went into business together, and we've been partners more or less ever since.'

'You and Eugene in business together – now that I'd like to see. What do you do?'

'Don't laugh,' said Mike. 'We've done well together. We started off designing computer systems for businesses – you know, helping them get set up – and then moved into training for their staff and maintenance for the systems we installed.'

'Please tell me Eugene does the technical stuff,' said Katie.

'Of course,' said Mike, 'although there's not so much of that these days, and what there is we have more than enough people to cover.'

'So what did you bring to this wonderful business you have together?'

'Well, in the early days Eugene would tell me about all these fantastic things his processors could do, but he had no idea what possible use they could be. You can imagine him, can't you? He was so out there – every day he'd be coming to me with some incredible development he'd read about, but without a clue as to what it might actually mean.'

'And that's where you came in?'

'More or less,' said Mike. 'Eugene was often bitterly disappointed by the mundane things I'd ask him to produce. You just had to look at any business, whether it was retail or transport or manufacturing, or banking even – they were all so desperate for new systems to help do the simplest of tasks. It's difficult to think back now to just how hopeless people felt when it came to computers.'

'And you were there to put their minds at rest? God help them!'

'No, that's not fair. I'd look at their business and suggest ways in which we could help. Eugene gave them the confidence to hire us, because they could see he was a whizz, and I was able to explain what Eugene could do in a language they could understand. I had to laugh when Eugene and I were implementing systems to allow real-time banking – you know, put your money in an account in London and withdraw it two seconds later in Manchester. Talk about poacher turned gamekeeper.'

'You don't say,' said Katie. 'Once again the banking

world is in the hands of Mike Maguire – it's a terrifying thought.'

'Aren't you ever tempted to do just one last fraud?' asked Mike. 'Surely it'd be easy for you to transfer huge amounts into a private account somewhere?'

Katie thought for a moment that might be why Mike was here – to suggest some crazy scheme to steal a load of money.

'That's just the point,' she said. 'It would be one final fraud, and then they'd put me in jail. I think we did enough of that for one lifetime, don't you?'

'Maybe so,' said Mike. 'Maybe so.'

Once again, they were both quiet; neither wanted to get on to Vegas just yet.

'Did you ever get married?' asked Katie after a while. Mike nodded.

'Yes, I did,' he said. 'I got married just after I moved back to Manchester.'

'So it didn't take you that long to get over me?' asked Katie, and smiled.

'I guess not,' said Mike. 'Not when you look at it like that.'

'What's her name? And are you still married?'

'Her name's Margaret and yes, we're still married.'

'And you knew her before you met me, yes?'

'Was it that obvious?' asked Mike.

'Well, it figures,' said Katie. 'You never really chased after anyone else in Manchester, and that's a pretty short time to meet someone and get married – that would have been some rebound. Do you love her?'

'Yes. Yes, I do.'

'That's good then,' said Katie.

'And you – did you ever meet anyone? Did you ever get married?'

Katie looked at Mike. 'No,' she said, 'I never met anyone. I spent my life yearning after some guy I knew in college, but I let him slip through my fingers. And now I find after all these years that he was two-timing me all along – can you believe that?'

'Now that's not fair – ' began Mike.

'Don't worry,' said Katie. 'I'm only winding you up. I'm still on my own and you know that's the way I like it, so it looks as though we both got what we were looking for, yes?'

'I guess so,' he said, and reached for his drink. Mike noticed that Katie had finished her vodka and orange. 'Would you like another?'

'No, thanks,' she said. 'Another one of those and I'll be in bits. That hit the spot, though, thank you.'

Katie waited a moment, and then asked Mike what she'd come to find out.

'So,' she said, 'are you going to tell me why you needed to call me? Why you had to break our agreement after all these years?'

'I owe you an explanation,' said Mike, 'I know. And I'm sorry I had to do this, especially if it disrupts what you have going here, but I'll say what I have to say and then I'll be gone, I promise. And I really do need your help.'

'Go on,' said Katie, coolly.

'Bruno never collected on his money,' said Mike.

'That doesn't surprise me,' said Katie. 'Is that the thing that's bugging you?'

'The thing that's bugging me is I can't understand why. Whatever he decided to do, he was going to need that money at some point. But he never did.'

'Well, he was an adult,' said Katie, 'even if he didn't always behave like one. I can't imagine he ever rationally decided what to do; he just did what he did without ever thinking. He knew how to get hold of his money; he just had to be sober enough to get around to it.'

'Did you ever see him again?' asked Mike. 'Once you'd left me in Vegas?'

'No, thank God! I flew home alone and was all the happier for it. Remember that stunt he pulled with the fork? That was only a part of it – he'd tried it on with me back at the hotel, and it wasn't very pleasant.'

'So what happened to him, then?' asked Mike.

'I don't know and I don't care, and I can't believe that after twenty years you're still feeling responsible for Bruno.'

'I don't feel responsible; I just want to know what happened to him.'

'Because you think it's going to come up when they go after you?'

'Partly, yes.'

'And how do you know he never touched it?' asked Katie. 'Does that mean you were keeping track of my money too?'

'I obviously knew where I'd put Bruno's money,' said Mike, 'so it was easy enough to check. I wanted to make sure he was okay. I knew you'd move your money right away, so there was little point in checking up on you. But the fact that Bruno's stash remained untouched was more worrying than if he'd blown it all within a month – in fact, I expected him to blow it all in a month.'

'All that money must be worth a fair bit by now,' said Katie.

'Well, yes,' said Mike, 'although not as much as if it had been managed from day one. I had to leave it where it was for a long while, just in case Bruno ever re-appeared to claim it; after several years though, it became obvious he wasn't coming back. I didn't like the idea of it just sitting there, easily traceable back to me and the Halibro share deal.'

'So you hid it?'

'Yes, I hid it and started investing it, so it would keep its value – just as you did with yours, I presume.'

'So, what's your problem?' asked Katie. 'If they can't trace your money, you'll get to keep it regardless of what they throw at you.'

'Bruno's money,' corrected Mike.

'Whatever,' said Katie. 'We both know he's not going to come looking for it now.'

'Do we?' asked Mike. 'I know he won't be able to find his money, but that won't stop him trying to find me.'

'Just like you found me?'

'I told you, that didn't take so much – I only had to open the newspaper.'

'And you read the Irish *Sunday Independent* at home, do you?' asked Katie. 'Bruno's not coming back, Mike; you know that. He'll have got into some scrape or other – you saw the state he was in that night. You knew he wouldn't last two minutes and he didn't. He was out of his depth in Vegas, and it's not the kind of place to suffer fools – or losers.'

'So what do you think happened to him?'

'Anything could have happened to him – what does it matter? He'll have been looking for drugs or something – why should we care?'

'I don't know how you can be so callous,' said Mike. 'He was our friend.'

'I'm not being callous,' said Katie; 'I'm being honest. He was your friend and I didn't like him. I hated having him around. I could never understand what you saw in his company, and I can't believe you still care.'

'You two were more alike than you chose to admit,' said Mike.

'Maybe so,' said Katie, 'and maybe that was the problem, but I don't care. I just don't care what happened to him, Mike, and if that's all you've come here to find out then I'm sorry, but I can't help you.'

'But if something had happened to him, there'd be a report of it somewhere. I know he never left the States – to this day I'm sure he's still listed as being illegally in the country – but how could he survive without money?'

'Jesus, Mike! How many times do I have to say it? I don't care. I don't care. I don't care!'

Katie had raised her voice and was attracting the attention of some people at the next table; she stared them down when they looked over.

'And what about me?' asked Mike. 'Do you care about me?'

'Of course I care about you,' said Katie, 'but I'm only just getting used to the idea that you're here. I've spent twenty years on my own, Mike; you can't just walk right back in and expect to pick up where we left off way back then.'

'I know and I'm sorry, and as I said, I didn't do it lightly – '

'Stop saying that! I don't care how lightly you did it – it's fucking with my head, that's all I know. I don't know what you think I might be able to do to help and, in fact, these were the very circumstances in which you said we shouldn't get in touch. All the lengths we went to – that you went to – to make sure there was no connection from me to the money from Halibro. Why bother, if at the first hint of trouble you come running to me?'

'There is no trouble,' said Mike.

'What?'

'There is no trouble. There's no FBI letter or a subpoena or an investigation. I just made that up to get you to meet me.'

'What?'

'Because I knew you wouldn't – '

'You fucking bastard, Mike! You fucking bastard.'

'Katie, I – '

'No, fuck off, Mike!' said Katie, and stood up. 'That's too much – you can't do that. What the fuck are you looking at?' she snapped at the couple on the next table. 'Is your own life so boring, you have to listen in on mine?'

The couple looked away again, not wanting to get involved.

'Katie,' said Mike.

'You've no right doing that, Mike, no right at all.'

'But you wouldn't have seen me otherwise.'

'And now I'm leaving,' said Katie. 'What difference did it make?'

'Please,' said Mike. 'I need to talk to you.'

'Tough!' said Katie. 'I've got absolutely no interest in anything you have to say – it'll all be lies, anyway.' She picked up her bag from the table. 'Don't contact me again, do you hear?'

'Katie,' said Mike again, but Katie was already walking away, putting on her coat as she made her way to the door. Mike stood up and went after her.

'Katie, please listen,' he said. 'I really do need your help – I don't know how else to put it, but I need your help.' He had to raise his voice to be heard across the foyer. 'Please.'

Katie stopped and turned around. There were more than just a couple of people watching and listening now but she didn't care. You don't choose the time or the place when your life becomes an entertainment for others; it was here and now in the foyer of the Gresham for Katie.

'You're a fucking bastard, Mike. You have no idea – '

'Yes, I do,' said Mike. 'I do have an idea and I'm sorry, but I needed to see you and I need your help.'

'How can you need my help?' asked Katie. 'And don't spin me another line – in fact, how can I believe a single word you say?'

'Please don't go, Katie,' said Mike. 'Please – and I'm sorry I had to do it this way – but please . . . Just don't go until you hear what I've got to say.'

'You'll lie to me.'

'I won't, I promise. That was a stupid thing to tell you this morning, but I was desperate and I didn't know how else to make sure you'd come.'

'You could have told me the truth.'

'I could,' said Mike, 'but you wouldn't have come. I promise I'll be straight with you now; I have to be because I need – '

'Because you need my help – you said that already.'

Katie looked at Mike. She breathed deeply but it wasn't a controlled breathing, more an attempt to cover her feelings.

'You've hurt me,' she said.

'I know, and I'm sorry.'

Nobody got close to Katie McGuire – so what was happening here?

Katie looked away to her left, towards the reception desk, and then back to her right, towards the bar. She looked back at Mike.

'If what we had means anything to you – ' he began.

'Don't you dare!' said Katie. 'Don't you fucking dare try to use what happened back then as a bargaining tool. You know I owe you everything; I owe my life to you and there's not a day goes by when I don't think of that so don't you dare try to tell me how much I'm in your debt.'

'Then listen to me now,' said Mike, 'because I need you.'

'How can you need me?' asked Katie.

'I need you and I'm begging you, please, not to go.'

The life of the foyer had begun to move on; they weren't quite the spectacle they had been a moment ago.

'Please, Katie.'

'You've hurt me,' said Katie again.

'I know,' said Mike, 'but that's not why I'm here. I don't want to upset you, but I do need to see you.'

'You hurt me just by being here.'

Katie felt herself unravelling – she felt the years being stripped away – and she didn't want to do this in public. She either walked or she stayed, but she had to decide quickly what to do.

Mike stepped towards her, but Katie stepped back.

'Don't!' she said, and Mike stopped. 'You're a fucking bastard, Mike.'

'Yes, you said.'

'A fucking bastard.'

'Got it,' said Mike. 'But you love me, right?'

'I owe you,' said Katie. 'I owe you enough to listen to you, that's all.'

3

They chose another table, in the bar and away from the open foyer.

'I'm going to have to eat something,' said Mike.

'I'll have a pot of tea,' said Katie. 'If you order some sandwiches then I'll share them with you.'

Katie left Mike alone while she went to freshen up and to recover some of her lost composure. She studied herself in the mirror. Her clothes and her look said successful businesswoman. She wondered if anyone in the foyer had recognized her – had she become the stuff of gossip columns out there? She realized she'd been crying. She cursed Mike again for doing this to her. But there was nothing here Katie didn't already know – the front she put on to the world could collapse at any moment; it was hardly surprising if it had almost happened today. She splashed her face with cold water, dried her hands and walked back out to the bar.

'I need to tell you about my home and family,' said Mike, 'and then I think you'll see why I'm here.'

'No bullshit, then,' said Katie.

'No bullshit, I promise.'

'Because I can tell when you're lying.'

'No lying, and no bullshit – I promise,' said Mike again.

Their food and drinks arrived; Mike had a Guinness this time, as though it was now he that needed the drink to help calm him down. Katie was happy with her tea and helped herself to a sandwich.

Mike looked up at Katie. It was an unguarded moment, and Katie saw something. His still young face reminded her of the summer days when they used to drive out to the hills above Manchester; when Mike would be trying but failing to figure Katie out. He'd looked lost then, and he looked lost now.

'What is it?' she asked.

But then the look was gone, and Nice Guy Mike was back.

'You were right about my wife,' he said. 'I knew her all the time you and I were together at college though, of course, I wasn't married to her at the time. We weren't even seeing each other – not in that way, anyway – so it wasn't as though I was cheating on her. And you and I weren't exactly what you'd call going out together, were we?'

'When did you meet your . . . How long had you known Margaret?'

'We used to meet in the library after school,' said Mike. 'That was where we first saw each other, and I can't imagine we'd ever have met otherwise.'

'It's a good place to meet girls, a library,' said Katie. 'You can fool them into thinking you're intelligent, and they like that.'

'Well, the similarity did occur to me a year or so later when you came over to talk to me in the Law Library that time. But anyway, getting back to Margaret . . . It took a couple of months of staring across the tops of desks and then looking quickly away before either one of us had the nerve to speak to each other. And when it did happen, it was only because her friends egged Margaret on; I would never have had the courage to say hello. I used the library because to get to school I had to travel the whole way across town, so it was easier to stop off on the way home and get my work done there. I'd be knackered by the time I got home otherwise, and this way I was still in a studying frame of mind – in my uniform and everything.'

Katie smiled.

'What?' asked Mike.

'The thought of you in your school uniform. Did you have a little cap on your head?'

'No, I didn't.'

'What age were you?'

'I was just seventeen; Margaret was almost sixteen and studying for her O levels. I was about to take my As. And the uniform is relevant, because it told Margaret where I went to school. There were always two or three of her friends with her, giggling at Margaret for daring to talk to me. She used the library because there was no space to work at home, she said.'

'Now that I can understand,' said Katie.

'Well, yeah. I guess nobody loved their library as much as you did.'

'It was private,' said Katie, 'your own space even though you're in a very public place. I could never have studied for my exams otherwise – certainly not at Margaret's age – so I know what she was doing.'

'She said if I couldn't handle a couple of girls giggling,' said Mike, 'there wasn't much hope for me. What she meant was, I was going to come up against greater resistance than that if I wanted to carry on seeing her. Because it was Belfast, the easy way of looking at it was that she was a Catholic and I was a Protestant and, sure, that was there – I'm not denying it. But when you got right down to it – when it was just the two of us – it was the fact that I had money and she didn't. Or rather, that my family had money and her family didn't.'

'There's nothing like a rich person for not knowing the value of money,' said Katie.

'But it's not as though we were rich,' said Mike. 'We weren't poor, but we weren't so well off either. I was just a middle-class schoolkid, and even that wasn't the real me; it was my family that wasn't poor, my family that was middle class. I was a schoolboy and this was the first time I'd come across how money can affect how one person might look at another.'

'I'm with Margaret on this one,' said Katie. 'I can imagine you were unbearable.'

'But that's just it,' said Mike. 'If I'd ever thought about it at all, I was just some kid who was studying to go to college. And then suddenly I was being looked at like I was some freak from landed gentry or something.'

'You'd have to be where Margaret was from to understand.'

'I know, I know,' said Mike, 'but this was a real lesson to me, the difference money makes to people's attitudes. And I don't mean the difference money makes to your life – I'm not that stupid, and I wasn't even that stupid back then. But Margaret looked at me differently because I wasn't poor; not necessarily any better or any worse than her – just different.'

'Again, I'm with Margaret here.'

'But it was just me,' insisted Mike.

'Just you, about to take your exams a year before anyone else, hoping to go to college to study law and definitely not hanging around Belfast for the rest of your life. What was Margaret hoping to do?'

'She's a nurse; she always knew she was going to be a nurse and that's what she did.'

'That's good, then,' said Katie.

'Yes, but the way she went about it shows what I mean. She was as desperate to leave Belfast as I was – or, at least, she claimed to be – and she could quite easily have gone away to college, even to Manchester, to study nursing and qualify over there.'

'But she left school at sixteen, went straight onto the ward, and stayed at home?'

'Exactly,' said Mike. 'And then for the rest of her life she has this hang-up about me having been to college and she never did and she wants it for our kids and can't understand when they don't want it too and it all goes back to money and how it makes you see your-self and the rest of the world.'

'You say you were only seventeen,' said Katie. 'Well,

cut her some slack. She was only sixteen at the time; maybe it was very difficult for her then. She moved over to Manchester eventually, didn't she?'

'Yes, yes, I guess so. I just hate that determination in some people to stay who they are, even when it doesn't do them any good.'

'You can't have hated it that much if you ended up marrying her,' said Katie.

'No,' said Mike, 'you're right. I'm just trying to give you as full a picture as possible, that's all.'

'From your point of view, you mean – I imagine Margaret's recollection differs slightly to yours.'

'I guess it does, but I can't speak for her so you're going to have to take me on trust. Jesus,' said Mike, 'you're a hard listener.'

Katie knew that Mike would have deliberated long and hard over the best approach to adopt in saying what he'd come to say – the best approach to get whatever it was he hoped to get out of Katie. The lost look she'd seen on Mike's face a few minutes earlier was the temptation simply to blurt it all out. Katie decided to give Mike the time and the space to tell it in his own way.

'Go on,' she said.

'After college – after Vegas – I went home. And yes, I know that was a luxury some people don't have; I was able to take my time to figure out what I wanted to do next. I had my parents, a family and a home where I could hang around, and do nothing much. Of course, I got some grief about giving up on the banking scholarship, and why had I studied law if I wasn't going to be a solicitor? But generally they were very understanding; I was taking my time before making my big decision.'

'*The Graduate*?' said Katie.

'Yeah, like that,' agreed Mike, 'only more so because, although both my parents are Irish, they've never lost that American drawl way of speaking. And they picked up that hard-nosed attitude to the professions while they were over there – hence their joy when I went to study law.'

'But now you were turning into a waster?'

'Well, I was still only twenty-one, as I kept reminding them, and they did allow me the space and time – and I know that's incredibly privileged, and not many people would have that kind of family set-up, but that was me and that was how it was, so I can't help that.'

'I didn't say a word,' said Katie.

'No,' said Mike, 'you don't need to.'

'So what conclusions did you come to?'

'Well, there were no great startling revelations,' said Mike, 'if that's what you mean. I thought about what I'd been up to over the previous four years, and realized that a lot of it was bordering on illegal – '

'More than bordering on, I'd say.'

'Yes, yes – whatever. But I wondered where it had all come from, all this money thing. You know, this obsession with proving how easy it was to amass money, even if a lot of it was through dodgy deals and fraud and suchlike? But I had done some remarkable things.

That listings magazine, for example, is still going strong – maybe not in the same form, but it started out in life as my magazine, none the less.'

Katie nodded in agreement, and Mike continued. 'I knew how to read and play the stock market,' he said, 'and I know we didn't earn a fortune playing cards, but we did have a lot of fun and probably ended up even over the years, if you take away the trip to Vegas.'

There it was, thought Katie. Mike was about to come on to Vegas.

'I thought about that whole Halibro thing,' said Mike, 'and I just thought – what the hell have I been doing? Where did all this stuff come from? What was I trying to prove or achieve?'

'And did you find out?' asked Katie.

Mike laughed.

'No, not really,' he said. 'Only that I'd gradually been building up to it – getting to college at an early age, being a high achiever, that sort of thing – and I felt now that part of my life was over.'

'Mike Maguire finally grows up,' said Katie.

'And you were a part of what I was going through,' said Mike. 'I'd spent four years trying to figure you out, trying to get close to you – trying to get you to fall in love with me, even – and now that was over too. And the money thing – I realized it was a poor substitute for what I really wanted, and that it didn't really do it for me or for you, and so what was the point?'

'The point was,' said Katie, 'that I did appreciate the money, and I still do. I'll never lose sight of what it allowed me to do.'

'But I think I was looking to save you, or something,' said Mike, 'and the money wasn't going to do that. And I still don't even know what I was trying to save you from.'

'You saved me from a life of poverty,' said Katie, 'that's what you saved me from.'

'Not really. You'd already come away with first-class honours in a law degree; I think you'd have worked things out just fine. You know I don't mean that.'

'So what do you mean?' asked Katie.

'That I'd got the money, but I hadn't got the girl,' said Mike.

'You had Margaret,' Katie pointed out.

'I know, and I know this isn't doing her any favours, making it look like she was second best to you, because that's not how it was. I loved her all the way through this; I just couldn't see how we could be together. We were realistic about the distance thing – I was in Manchester and she was back in Belfast – and we knew it might not work out. There was every possibility that I would meet someone and she said that if I did, then that was okay.'

'And you believed she meant that?'

'At the time, yes, because I was so young, but I can see with hindsight that she may just have been saying it. And I did meet someone, didn't I? And whatever you may think of yourself, Katie, I knew how I felt about you and, yes, I wanted to save you and be the one to make your life okay.'

'But then you realized I was a hopeless case – am a hopeless case?'

'Yes, basically,' said Mike, 'but I never thought of you exactly in those terms. I could see that you couldn't be with me and that nothing I could do or say, or no amount of money I could throw at the problem, was ever going to make any difference; so I had to just walk away.'

'That's what I told you at the time,' said Katie, 'only, unlike Margaret, I meant what I said.'

'But you're a hard act to follow,' said Mike. 'And again, I know I'm being unfair to Margaret, because I really did love her all this time and I fancied her like mad and I still do, but, to tell you the truth, it was just – '

'That you'd met me and I'd messed with your head?'

'Yes,' said Mike. 'Yes.'

'I'm sorry.'

'Well don't be, because I'm not. To this day I'm glad I got to know you then and that you were a part of my life, even if you couldn't stay a part of it forever.'

'The feeling's mutual,' said Katie, 'for what it's worth.'

Katie felt good to be able to sit here and say this to Mike.

'Tell me about Margaret,' she said.

'Yes . . . Margaret,' said Mike.

'And I don't want any "My wife doesn't understand me" bullshit, either.'

'No, that's not why I came,' said Mike. 'I know I'm

216

a weird fuck, so I can't complain when people don't understand me.'

Katie laughed.

'What's so funny?' asked Mike. 'Don't you believe me?'

'No, it's nothing,' said Katie. 'Somebody called me just that – a weird fuck – only this morning.'

'Well, you are – or were at any rate – and twice as bad as I ever was.'

'Go on,' said Katie.

Mike picked up his glass and finished off his pint. He poured out some of the iced water that had come with the sandwiches.

'As I said, I fancy Margaret like mad. That might seem self-evident to you, but I keep on going back to it because I see so many men my age living with women who they just don't want. Whatever they once had, if they ever had it, they don't have it anymore. And I'm not claiming there haven't been times – phases, if you like – when I lost sight of that with Margaret, but I'm proud of the fact that I fancy my wife.'

'You really are a weird fuck,' said Katie.

'Yeah, well, you can imagine what she was like as a teenager – very, very sexy, dirty even.'

'Spare me, please.'

'Anyway, when it came right down to it, once I'd got over my moody return from college and my not knowing what I was going to do, Margaret understood that eventually I'd work my way back to her. She didn't know about you, though she might have guessed there was someone, and she didn't know what my problem was with getting a job or earning a living or deciding where to live; but she knew that once I'd come to my senses, I'd see that I was meant to be with her. Does that sound conceited?'

'Not necessarily,' said Katie.

'It's meant to be a compliment – to Margaret – that she knew all along what she wanted and she was just waiting for me to come to the same conclusion. I think men are a bit slow sometimes, when it comes to things like that?'

'There's no one arguing with you here,' said Katie.

'We knew each other so well by then that when I finally realized what I wanted – as in to share my life and have a family with Margaret – it was simply a matter of where we would choose to live.'

'And so you moved back to Manchester?'

'Yes,' said Mike. 'Neither family was ecstatic about us getting married – even if they didn't actively try to dissuade us – but we knew we had to set up on our own elsewhere, and Manchester was where I knew best. And learnt to love, it has to be said. I had enough money for us to move over and buy a small place to live – '

'You see,' interrupted Katie. 'There you go again. Young college graduates of twenty-one don't have enough money to buy their own place, just because they decide that's what they want to do.'

'But it was all my money: what I'd earned from the stock market, mainly, and that was it – all gone; there was no more. I'd made my big decision about Margaret, but for the life of me I still couldn't think about how I was going to work for a living. And the more Margaret went on about it, the less inclined I was to do anything. I knew I had to do something, but I just couldn't come up with any bright ideas.'

'You could have got a job, like the rest of the world.'

'I know,' said Mike, 'but for some reason I think I wanted to live through a little poverty for a while.'

'Like a tourist,' said Katie.

'Yes, like a tourist, but also because I'd seen where money had got me in the past – absolutely nowhere – and now I felt like it was all that was expected of me.'

'So you were a contrary little bastard?' said Katie. 'I can imagine that went down well with Margaret?'

'She was concerned all right – more than concerned, actually. I think she wondered what the hell she'd got herself into, especially because she was pregnant at the time.'

'That would focus her mind all right, I'd have thought.'

'Yes, and it focused mine too,' said Mike, 'but I still didn't know what to do. I'm only talking about a few months or so, but Margaret found it tough being away from home, in a foreign city – '

'And being married to a waster who'd never had to work in his life?'

'I guess so.'

'And it was Eugene who came to your rescue?'

'Yes, Eugene.'

'Is he well?' asked Katie. 'And happy?'

'You wouldn't recognize him, Katie – he's so sure and confident of himself. He's just . . . I don't know, he's a good friend.'

'That's good.'

'Of course,' said Mike, 'straight after college, he was still just Eugene, and I only saw him socially a couple of times to let him know I was back in Manchester. He was doing research at the university – in maths – but he'd become a computer freak and that's all he'd talk about when we met. But he had absolutely no idea of the practical applications of what he was talking about.'

'Whereas the great Mike Maguire, of course . . .'

'Well, I didn't just dive in and tell him what he should be doing, but at one point he was responsible for the interviewing of applicants to study maths, and he showed me the spreadsheet he had set up. So I asked about how sophisticated all the college systems were for things like registration and timetables and budgets, and it seemed everything was fairly haphazard – the odd enthusiast like Eugene working on their own, but there was not one whole integrated system.'

'And you persuaded them you were the man for the job?'

'No, I persuaded them it needed doing and that my company was capable of doing it.'

'And your company was?'

'Myself and Eugene.'

'You're a fucking chancer, Mike.'

'Not really. I knew Eugene could do it, and I was right.'

'So you were on your way, back in business?' asked Katie.

'More or less,' said Mike. 'Eugene didn't give up his day job for a while, but eventually we became so busy and were making so much money that I persuaded him it was for the best.'

'And was he happy to give up on his maths?'

'I think so; he liked the challenge of each new project we took on and did all the programming himself for the first few years. He just switched his energies from one thing to the other.'

'And found a practical way of using his brain in the world?'

'Yes,' said Mike. 'I think so. If Eugene helped me back then – which he did, enormously – I think I helped him too. Of course, he could have stayed doing research forever, but I think he liked what we did. It changed again when we switched more to managing and maintaining the systems we'd installed, or other systems that businesses had bought with absolutely no support. At first I dealt with the clients and relayed the problems back to Eugene, but he gradually became involved on site and more socially adept at dealing with people. As I said – you wouldn't recognize him now.'

'And meanwhile you were becoming a daddy?' asked Katie.

'Yes, and I have to say, as soon as I did then everything fell into place for me. Again, I guess Margaret knew how it would be all along, but I had to be shown. I hadn't realized that this was the point of everything.'

'It's what they say,' said Katie.

'And it's true, it's true,' said Mike. 'You know the Bob Dylan song – "Sara"? Well, it's a bit soppy, I know, but there's a line in it about being on the beach with his wife while the kids play in the sand, and it just seems to be so what it's all about. You're there with your partner and you love her and want her, and the kids are happy, but there's always one of them demanding your attention, so you don't actually have much time to yourselves; but you know that when you do it's going to be nice and so you spend a lot of your time anticipating being alone together rather than being together, but it's still good.'

'How many children do you have?'

'Three – two boys and a girl. Jack, Mike and Katherine; they're not kids anymore, though. Jack will be twenty this year.'

'Fucking hell, Mike!'

'Fucking hell is right – you look around and another decade's gone by. You just remember snapshots of each one at different ages, but you're so damn busy all the time, you end up wondering just where all the years have gone. It might be a cliché, but it's an accurate one.'

'So you became a responsible parent?' said Katie.

'Yes,' said Mike, but he didn't continue. He shook the almost melted ice around the bottom of his empty glass of water.

'What?' asked Katie.

Mike took his time to reply.

'Yeah,' he said, 'I became a responsible parent. For years I was the sole wage earner and that, as you said, focuses your mind all right. You forget any fancy notions or crazy ideas, and you certainly forget about doing anything that might border on illegal. You make sure the next contracts are signed and that the work doesn't dry up, and that was tough enough in the eighties, I can tell you. A lot of people still didn't really trust computers, or what they could do for your business. We had to wait quite a while before we were proven right – before it became obvious that, just to survive, every business was going to have to install some form of system. And of course by then everybody was at it so we had to reinvent ourselves all over again.'

'But you managed, from the sound of it?'

'Yes,' said Mike, 'but it was no fun, and I didn't like what it was doing to me. I was losing something – I was losing the bit of me that I liked.'

'But you'd become someone Margaret could trust and depend upon?'

'Yes, but this is the thing – I don't think she liked what I'd become either. Only in a way I was her creation. I'd done what she wanted, made our life secure and, yes, I had become someone she could depend upon.'

'But she missed her Mike?'

'I missed her Mike! I told you I wouldn't go on about Margaret, and I'll try not to, and I can't speak for how she felt or when she felt it, but I do know what I was thinking at the time.'

'Which was what?' asked Katie.

'Well, the thing that made sense of everything for me, as I said, was being a parent. And, as I keep on saying, I was still relatively young. You grow up yourself as a kid and then all of a sudden you're this conscious being, wondering what the fuck it's all about. And I think that's what happened to me after college because I knew it wasn't just about the money; I knew it wasn't just about getting high and having a good time; and I knew that some things just can't be put right, no matter what you throw at them. I knew all these incredible people – '

'Remarkable people,' said Katie.

'Exactly,' said Mike, 'remarkable people. But I didn't know what the fuck I was doing on the planet. And then one day this tiny thing that you've watched being born, this eating, shitting and sleeping machine – sleeping if you're lucky, that is – looks up at you and recognizes you and smiles. And it might be just wind making him smile but it doesn't matter, because he follows you with his eyes and you might be just a shape but that doesn't matter either because you're his shape and he likes you – loves you, actually, unconditionally and without question.'

'You liked being a dad, then?' asked Katie.

'I did, yes,' said Mike, 'and I do, but what I'm saying is this: if I'd wanted an answer to what the hell I was doing on the planet, I was given one fairly immediately.'

'And you were still only twenty-one?'

'Yes,' said Mike. 'I didn't mind at first where my new responsibilities were taking me, because I was learning to be a dad.'

'And then?'

'And then pretty much the same for quite a few years, well into the nineties. We were fairly well off by this stage – '

'Legitimately!'

'Yes, legitimately, and also because Margaret had returned to work, so we had two wages coming in.'

'So you started having fancy notions again?' asked Katie.

'No, amazingly,' said Mike. 'I just carried on the same old same old, which I think now was a mistake but at the time I thought was the right thing to do. Having the kids was not so easy for Margaret – it's not that glamorous being stuck at home all the time and I didn't always have that much to contribute on the rare times I might be around. I guess it was Margaret's time for wondering just what the fuck it's all about. So when she started back at work I thought we were getting through the rough patch, that once she was back in the workplace she'd get back some of her self-worth.'

'And she didn't?'

'Only up to a point,' said Mike. 'I thought if I just encouraged her it would be enough; I guess she needed more from me than that. And there was something else going on at the time too.'

Mike poured himself the remaining water from the

jug on the table. 'Are you okay for a drink?' he asked Katie.

'I'm fine, thanks. Go on.'

'The kids were growing up – which you'll probably say is obvious, but it's not so obvious when you're right in the middle of it. When they're really young, you struggle on from one phase to the next – especially with your first kid – and just when you come to terms with where they're at, they've moved on to the next phase. The second time around you recognize things a lot quicker, and by the third you're an old pro. We now had two teenage sons, which was hard enough but nothing too tragic – the odd scare was all. But then Jack was about to leave school – '

'And Margaret was desperate for him to go to college, and you didn't care one way or the other?'

'Yes,' agreed Mike. 'We went through all that and it was as you describe, but we got over it. The point was, Jack was going; he was leaving home. He tried college at first but really what he was doing was leaving home. And I don't think Margaret had thought that through.'

'What do you mean?'

'Well, it's kind of accepted, isn't it, that mothers love their children more than they love their partners?'

'Is it?' asked Katie.

'Put it this way, every bloke knows it's true. It's never said out loud but when it gets right down to it, given the choice, mothers would go with their kids every time. And that's fair enough because most partners are a waste of space anyway, I know, but what happens when the kids leave home? The mothers are left with the horse they didn't back.'

'So Jack was gone . . .'

'And it was pretty obvious Mike junior wouldn't be far behind. He couldn't wait to be either travelling or earning, or both.'

'And Margaret was left with you and Katherine, and the feeling that life was passing her by.'

'Yes,' said Mike.

'And now you're thinking the same? That once Katherine leaves, the two of you are going to be strangers to one another?'

'It's possible,' said Mike. 'I hope it doesn't work out that way, but the thought has occurred to me.'

'And so now you're thinking, did I make the right choice all those years ago? What if I'd stayed with Katie? Would my life have been so very different? Fucking hell, Mike, this is just midlife crisis nonsense and you know it. Please tell me you didn't bring me here for that – you know we could never have been together. We wouldn't have lasted twenty minutes, and here you are married to Margaret for over twenty years.'

Mike put down his glass and smiled.

'No,' he said, 'I didn't bring you here for that. I loved you, Katie, you know that, and I think I was right to love you, but I don't think that's the answer to my problems. I'm here for a very different reason altogether.'

'A few years ago,' said Mike, 'Margaret had sex with another man. She says it was just a one-off thing and

I believe her. It hurt me a lot at the time and it still hurts me now, but I can see why it happened and that's why I just told you all that shit. I can't say I handled it well – I don't know how to measure these things – and I was in a bad way there for a long time. But the way I feel now is, I love Margaret and I want us to be together. I don't think it will be easy, but I think that's the only hope I have of making sense of my life again.

'The way Margaret feels is different. I think she hates herself and can't get over what she's done. I don't think I helped by going off at the deep end like I did, but I couldn't stop that at the time. Maybe some couples can brush this off, but I couldn't and now Margaret can't.'

Mike paused for a moment.

'C'est la vie, you might think,' he said. 'Tough shit; get over it! There's no reason why everything should be okay just because I want it to be. I wouldn't argue with you about that.

'Margaret's reaction has been different to mine: it's been to shut down her feelings and to not let me in. She's put all her energy elsewhere – into her work and her studies – because, after all, that's the direction her life was heading anyway. But I don't want to live my life in that way.'

Mike was quiet again for a moment, and Katie didn't speak.

'That's okay for the grown-ups,' he said. 'A couple of idiots who have fucked up the one good thing they had together – we deserve all we get. But it's not okay for our daughter, for Katherine.

'She kind of got lost in all of this, but I don't think any of it was lost on her. You think you're being so sophisticated, keeping your fights and your arguments and your storming out for when she's up in bed, but of course she doesn't miss a thing. And my solution was to find reasons to be away from the house for days at a time, as though she couldn't see through what was really going on.'

'What age is she?' asked Katie quietly.

'She'll be fifteen this year,' said Mike.

'And you and Margaret have been fighting for what – three or four years?'

'There've been good times in there as well,' said Mike, 'but yes, it's about that – longer, actually.'

'So a third of your daughter's life has been spent with her parents falling apart?'

'Tearing each other apart would be a more accurate description,' said Mike.

'And her brothers left home during this time as well?'

'Yes,' said Mike.

Katie didn't need to tell Mike what he and Margaret had done; she could see he knew well enough.

'It would have been better if you'd left,' she said eventually.

'I know,' said Mike, 'but I couldn't. I tried, and I couldn't. That's how I'm so sure now that I want us to be together.'

'It takes two for that to work,' said Katie.

'Yes, I know.'

'Three maybe, in this case.'

Katie thought of herself at fifteen, and all she could remember was confusion. She always considered her conscious life as an adult to have begun once she was allowed to leave school; anything before that was just a chance rebounding from one nightmare situation to the next. There are happy childhoods and there are unhappy childhoods, but you have no control over which you get.

'You came here to tell me about your daughter,' she said.

'Yes,' said Mike. 'Or, at least, to ask you about her.'

'She's your daughter, Mike,' said Katie. 'You can start by telling me something good about her, something I'm going to like.'

Mike cleared his throat.

'Well,' he said, 'you know I'm going to tell you that she's beautiful – and she is – but she's more than that. She's sharp and clever and funny and unique. She's the perfect opposite in many ways to Jack and Mike – not that they aren't those things too – but she is just so completely her own person. I guess she had her brothers there to help bring her along, so she's savvy and street-smart and wise beyond her years. She's . . . what? What can I say? I love her; she's my daughter.'

'That would do it,' said Katie, and smiled; though she knew there was nothing much here to smile about.

'She's very sick,' said Mike.

'I thought she might be,' said Katie. 'And that's why you're here?'

'Yes.'

'You'd better tell me,' said Katie. 'Tell me what she's doing to herself.'

Please don't let it be cutting, thought Katie. Please don't let it be cutting.

'She's refusing to eat,' said Mike. 'She . . . she just won't eat anything.'

'For how long?' asked Katie.

'For nearly four weeks now.'

'And before that?' asked Katie. 'Was she trying it out before that?'

'We don't know,' said Mike. 'We don't think so but we can't be sure. If you've got a teenage daughter, then you watch out for these things but really, if she wanted to hide it from us, then it would have been easy.'

'You mean yourself and Margaret were too busy fighting to notice?'

'No, not really, no,' said Mike. 'That's the thing – the house has been better recently. I'm not saying I don't have moments when I lose it – when I go off to my room like a little boy because I get so upset – but we don't fight anymore, and the house is generally pleasant and calm.'

'But Katherine could . . . she could have been thinking about this for a long time?' asked Katie.

'Knowing Katherine,' said Mike, 'then yes, I think she's deliberately set out to do this. I don't think she's just fallen into it by chance. The doctors believe she must have been experimenting before.'

'I'd say she could get away with anything if she

wanted to,' said Katie, 'and I don't mean simply because you and Margaret were too preoccupied to notice. Teenage girls find a way when they want to. If it makes you feel any better, I doubt this is all down to you and Margaret.'

'Thanks,' said Mike. 'I mean thanks for saying that, but I think you're wrong. I know what the doctors tell me, but I don't believe this is an eating disorder; I think it's a protest against myself and Margaret for letting her down.'

'Perhaps every eating disorder has its roots in some form of protest,' said Katie, 'and then ends up just being what it is.'

'That's what they told us at the hospital – not necessarily a protest, but some form of . . . anything, really. Whatever grievance she had before just doesn't matter anymore. But they don't know Katherine like I do; she knows exactly what she's doing to us by doing this to herself.'

'She probably blames herself more than she blames you,' said Katie. 'Is she very weak?'

'She's barely conscious,' said Mike. 'She . . . There isn't enough of her to have any kind of resistance.'

'Will she talk to you?'

'No,' said Mike. 'She's refused to talk to me or her mother.'

'What – she hasn't spoken in all that time?'

'That's right,' said Mike. 'And now I don't know whether she can't talk to us, or she won't. She's just slipping away.'

'What do the doctors say?' asked Katie. 'Do they think she can she still hear you?'

'Yes,' said Mike. 'They say I should never stop talking to her – not that I would anyway – but again I don't know whether she can't hear me or won't listen to me.'

'You mean she might still be deliberately ignoring you?'

'Yes,' said Mike.

'So what's to be done?' asked Katie. 'Can they force-feed her? I don't know what happens – she couldn't just die, surely?'

Katie regretted her choice of words as soon as she'd said them. Mike looked away, across the room to the bar.

'They can give her supplements,' he said, 'and she's on a drip. And they've had various attempts at giving her something more substantial, but they didn't have much success and it wasn't pretty to watch. So yes, if something doesn't happen soon, she'll slip into a coma and die.'

'And is she capable of eating anything by herself?' asked Katie.

'I don't know,' said Mike. 'And the doctors don't know either – whether she's capable and refusing, or past the point where she can help herself. Sooner or later though, she's going to reach that point.'

'But you don't think she's there yet?'

'I hope she isn't. I hope that if she really wanted to, she could find a way to pull herself out of this.'

'But for now she's determined not to?'

'That's about the size of it,' said Mike. 'And I'm running out of things to say to her that I think might change her mind.'

'I'm sorry,' said Katie. 'I'm really sorry.'

'I don't believe . . .' Mike began. 'I can't believe that she really wants to die. But I'm scared now that she's got no control over it one way or the other.'

Katie said nothing because there was nothing to say.

'I should have said stubborn,' said Mike. 'When I was describing her to you, I forgot to tell you how stubborn she can be.' He wiped away his tears with the heels of his hands. 'But this surely is taking the piss?'

'She wants to teach you a lesson,' said Katie.

'That's some fucking lesson,' said Mike. 'Enough, already.'

'She'll decide when it's enough.'

'But I can't believe,' said Mike, 'I can't believe she'd deliberately kill herself just to make sure we got the message. I know I've hurt her, and I know she's hurting, but what kind of a mind can see it through for that long?'

'A determined one,' said Katie. 'But you're right not to give up – she's depending on you for that.'

'I don't know what to think or believe.'

'You can believe that she needs you,' said Katie. 'And that she needs her mother.'

Mike looked away.

'Where's Margaret in all of this?' asked Katie.

Mike didn't reply. Katie gave him a minute or two, but he still said nothing.

'Mike,' said Katie, 'what about Margaret? Tell me about Margaret.'

Mike looked up at Katie and then away again.

'Mike!'

'Margaret refuses to go and see Katherine,' he said eventually. 'She refuses to talk about Katherine, or to accept that this is happening. She's shut herself down completely where Katherine is concerned.'

'Oh Mike,' said Katie, and then, 'Oh God.'

'Exactly,' said Mike.

'Because she thinks she's to blame?'

'You'd have to ask her that,' said Mike. 'Not that she's likely to answer you at all.'

'But surely she understands what's happening? Where this is going?'

'I guess she does,' said Mike, 'but it's not enough to change her mind.'

'Oh God,' said Katie again.

'What kind of a person could do that, do you think?' asked Mike. 'What kind of a mother could shut herself off from her own daughter?'

Katie excused herself and went to the bathroom. She had to get away from Mike to think at all clearly about this. She looked at herself in the mirror. She was alone in the room.

Poor Mike, she thought. Mike Maguire, and the women in his life.

'Poor Katherine,' she said out loud.

And poor Margaret. Katie couldn't begin to think what Margaret might be going through.

She returned to Mike.

'I forgot to tell you,' said Mike, when Katie sat down, 'though you might already have guessed. I named Katherine after you. No one else knows – except perhaps Eugene – because they don't need to know, and it wouldn't make any sense to tell them anyhow. But I know, and it's important to me, for what it's worth. I had hoped to be able to tell you some day. Not like this though; I didn't picture it ever being like this.'

'What about your sons?' asked Katie. 'Are they not old enough to help out?'

'They are,' said Mike, 'but I'm not sure I want them to see their sister in the state she's in.'

'But they're going to have to be told,' said Katie. 'And sooner rather than later, I'd have thought.'

'I know, but it's got to the point where I don't know what's best to do about telling Jack and Mike junior. I'm sure if I told them that Katherine was sick, they'd both want to come home.'

'And is that such a bad thing?' asked Katie. 'Why have you left it so long?'

'Because Margaret asked me not to get in touch with them,' said Mike. 'She didn't want the two boys to be dragged into our arguments, and I . . . I thought she was right – or at least I did at the time. Now I'm not so sure what to do.'

'If Katherine's as sick as you say,' said Katie, 'you're going to have to let them know, and fuck whatever Margaret might think.'

'I agree,' said Mike, 'only it's still difficult to go against Margaret's wishes, even if I don't necessarily agree with her. Plus, I wanted to speak to you first.'

Yes, but why? thought Katie. Why?

'Mike,' she said, 'I'm flattered that you should want to tell me. And I'm sorry to hear about your daughter, really sorry.'

Mike shrugged.

'I don't know why you had to go about it in such a crazy way,' said Katie, 'but then that's you all over. Perhaps you're right. I might have refused to see you if you'd told me straight out why you were here. Whatever. It's done now, and I'm glad you came; but I don't know what else I can do for you. There's nothing I can say that would make it any better. You need to be with your daughter, Mike, in Manchester, and not here in Dublin with me.'

'I'll be back there soon enough,' said Mike. 'I appreciate you agreeing to meet me – I know it wasn't easy. And listening to me – there aren't many people I can talk to about this, apart from Katherine's doctors of course.'

Mike hesitated for a second or two.

'I have something else to ask of you, though,' he said. 'Something more than just listening.'

'I'm not sure what else I can do for you here,' said Katie.

'It's not here that I'm looking for your help,' said Mike. 'I want you to come back with me to Manchester and talk to Katherine.'

Katie looked at Mike. 'I wouldn't be able to do that,' she said.

'That's what I came here to ask,' said Mike.

'Well then, no. I'm sorry, but no.'

'Any particular reason?'

'I don't need a reason,' said Katie. 'I just can't, is all – and I don't know what good you think it might do. I don't know Katherine and she doesn't know me. If she won't respond to you, she's hardly likely to respond to me.'

'I think she might,' said Mike.

'Because you're desperate,' said Katie, 'but you're wrong. She needs you and she needs her mother, not some stranger she's never met. She needs her mother.'

'She hasn't got her mother.'

'Her brothers, then,' said Katie. 'And if you can't bring yourself to ask them, she's going to need her father all the more. Look, Mike, if I've helped by being here – '

'You have.'

'But you have to get back to Katherine now. What did you think I could do?'

Mike was about to reply, but Katie carried on speaking. 'I don't know what you thought this might have to do with me. It's mixed up in your head with the regrets over your marriage. So you want out of whatever mess you and Margaret are in. Fine, but you know I'm not the answer. I wasn't right for you back then, and I wouldn't be right now. As I said, I'm flattered that you thought to come looking for me, but you've got to get back to your daughter. Go home, Mike. Go home now, before it's too late.'

'That's not why I'm here, Katie,' said Mike. 'I loved you then and, seeing you now, I think I could love you still; but that's not why I'm here. I'll say it again: I want you to come back to Manchester with me and talk to Katherine.'

'I'm not going back to Manchester,' said Katie.

'You know why I'm asking you,' said Mike.

'No, I don't know. Tell me why.'

'Because I think you know of a way to reach Katherine.'

'Why would I know of a way to reach Katherine when you can't?'

'I don't know,' said Mike, 'and you know I don't know, and you can hide behind that if you want to, but you know why I'm asking you and you know why I think you can help.'

'I don't know what you mean,' said Katie. 'You're talking in riddles.'

'Okay then,' said Mike, 'here it is in plain English – from an Irishman living in England to an English-woman living in Ireland. You've been living through some pain your whole life and I don't know what that pain might be. I hoped I could save you from that pain and I failed, and now I think I'm going to fail Katherine in the very same way that I failed you.'

Katie didn't speak.

'Whatever the pain is that you've been going through,' said Mike, 'I think it could help you to reach my daughter.'

Katie still didn't speak.

'You're right,' said Mike, 'I am desperate. But desperate people do desperate things. I don't know why I believe this might help Katherine, but I do.'

He sat and waited for an answer.

'You didn't fail,' said Katie, eventually.

4

Margaret had anticipated finishing her morning session in Alderley Edge, and then having lunch in Didsbury on her way to the afternoon appointment in Withington. It made sense in terms of the travel involved. It would also have kept her busy and on the move; the last thing she wanted to do was languish at home. But because she had left home in a hurry – grabbing the opportunity and excuse to avoid Eugene – she now had to drive all the way back to pick up what she needed for the afternoon.

Margaret took the motorway and resigned herself to her change of plan. The drive gave her time to assess how her morning session had gone. She felt drained – as she always did after counselling – and could quite easily have fallen into a deep sleep. She worried sometimes how it was possible to slip into the traffic of three or four lanes of motorway and not even think about the mechanics of driving. She could travel for ten or fifteen miles and not remember making a single conscious decision to take this exit or merge with that lane. Every now and again, Margaret would resolve to concentrate only on driving, but it was so monotonous that she couldn't keep it up for longer than a minute. She knew it was dangerous, and wondered how many other cars were being driven in this way.

Her client in Alderley Edge was unusual in that he was a man. It wasn't that men didn't need counselling; it was just unusual for a man to actually seek it out. Especially in a case such as this: the man's partner was the sole wage earner and was not prepared to accept that his self-esteem might have been threatened by the reversal in roles. He was in his late forties and couldn't get back into the work habit after having been made redundant; he was doing volunteer work at the local charity shop, which he believed his partner privately thought was ridiculous. Her career had gone from strength to strength once the children were grown, and he'd become obsessed with the possibility that she was having an affair at work.

Margaret had seen him three times now. She'd immediately recommended joint counselling, but the man's partner wasn't interested. Margaret knew this was a major obstacle if they hoped to resolve their differences together – so much so that today she'd switched away from that approach altogether.

'I think you have to focus on what is right for you,' she said. 'If you can't work this out together, you're going to have to do it on your own.'

Margaret liked the man, and could see he had a lot of things going for him. His decision to do charity work while he got back on his feet was a positive thing, she thought – easily dismissed, but it showed he had at least some self-worth.

'I wouldn't normally put it in exactly this way,' she said, 'but I think you have to be prepared to accept that you might be better off alone.'

Margaret's client looked up sharply when she said this.

'I know my job here is to help you find a way to make your relationship work,' she said, 'but there's very little point in having a relationship with someone who doesn't care about how you feel.'

Margaret thought about this in her car on the motorway. She'd have to write this up clearly and make sure she was taking the right approach. Had she overstepped the line in guiding rather than accompanying her client? She'd have to ask when she was next in college.

Margaret turned off the motorway, headed into Stretford, and then on to Longford Park. She drove along her road and looked to see if there was space to park outside the house. She was irritated to see Eugene's BMW parked two houses down and Eugene in it, sat waiting for her return. Driving into an empty space, she did it badly and was mad at herself for not reversing in properly. She left her notes from the morning on the seat beside her, picked up her bag and got out of the car. She walked across the road, into her front garden, and up the few steps to the door.

'Margaret,' said Eugene from the gateway.

'Eugene,' said Margaret, and unlocked the door. She spoke without turning around. 'You can be arrested for less, you know.'

'I . . . I –'

'Don't tell me,' said Margaret. 'You really want to speak to me.'

'Yes,' said Eugene.

'You'd best come in then, but I warn you – I'm on my way back out as soon as I have my stuff together.'

Margaret pushed open the front door and walked in the house. The kitchen was down a couple of steps at the end of the hallway, at a lower level to the rest of the house. She waited for Eugene to follow her inside, and then she closed the kitchen door. This was Margaret's domain – it was like a self-sufficient unit, a cocoon, and it seemed all the more so with her books spread out across the kitchen table.

'You've been studying,' said Eugene.

Margaret cleared away the coffee jug and cup from her morning's work in the kitchen. She didn't offer to make a drink; she'd have to get a bite to eat in Withington now.

'You're not at the hospital today then?' asked Eugene.

'You know I'm not,' said Margaret.

She started to gather up her books and files. She needed her project with her in case she had any spare time to work on it this afternoon. She picked up the file for the counselling session in Withington, and put everything into her college bag.

'What do you want, Eugene?' she asked. 'Why are you here?'

The years had been kind to Eugene – he still suffered from chronic shyness, but he'd lost the nerdiness he'd had in college and was no longer the geek he'd once been. He'd learnt how to dress well and his glasses were almost fashionable, or at least not so noticeable as they once had been, and he changed the frames every five years or so. He disagreed with the wearing of contact lenses as there was a lack of data on their long-term safety for the eyes. He'd put on a little weight, but he could afford to and he carried it well. He'd learnt how to handle himself in company, particularly in business situations, where Mike often left him on his own. He didn't come across so much as the freaky boffin these days, more the informed expert whose advice you'd appreciate and listen to. That was out in the world though; face to face and alone with Margaret was a different matter.

'I was looking for Mike,' he said.

'You tried that line this morning, remember? Let's not play games, Eugene.'

'Actually, I really am looking for Mike,' said Eugene. 'It's part of the reason I want to speak to you.'

'You know Mike's not here,' said Margaret, 'so stop pretending otherwise. I doubt if you'd have dared call unless you knew he wouldn't be here.'

'I know he's not here, but I don't know where he's gone,' said Eugene.

'I know where he told me he's gone,' said Margaret, 'but that doesn't necessarily mean I know where he is.'

'Would he lie to you?'

'It's what partners do to each other, Eugene – haven't

you heard? Didn't he let you know where he'd be today? He's your partner as well, after all.'

'He didn't say,' said Eugene. He looked at Margaret. 'You don't have to be so rude, you know.'

'Was I being rude?' asked Margaret. 'I'm sorry – Mike's gone to Dublin for the day. He'll be home late this evening. There – does that answer your question?' She fastened the buckle on her college bag and looked back at Eugene.

'Why would he go to Dublin?'

'I don't know, Eugene,' said Margaret. 'And if you don't know, it's obviously something he wants to keep from the two of us. There's nothing new here – surely you know by now that Mike enjoys his little secrets?'

'I mean,' said Eugene, 'why would he go to Dublin now, with everything that's going on?'

'You'd have to ask Mike that,' said Margaret.

'But there's nothing in Dublin but – '

Eugene stopped in mid-sentence; Mike had shown him the cuttings of Katie's articles in the *Sunday Independent* a few weeks ago.

'What?' asked Margaret. 'There's nothing in Dublin but what?'

'Nothing,' said Eugene.

He was obviously lying, but Margaret let it go. 'It's not the first time he's gone off without saying,' she said. 'Why should you be so concerned today?'

'Because I think he's had enough of me,' said Eugene. 'Of being in business with me, I mean.'

'And do you really need him any more?' asked

Margaret. 'Surely you could run the business on your own by now, without Mike?'

'We've so many people working for us,' said Eugene, 'all I do now is turn up to collect my wages — and I don't really need to do that to be paid. But at least I still show my face occasionally; Mike doesn't even bother turning up.'

'So what's the problem?' asked Margaret. 'You're making your money, the business is sound, and you have time on your hands. Learn to play golf or something — isn't that what you boys are supposed to do at this stage?'

'You're — you're not being very nice,' said Eugene. 'I don't want to play golf. I don't want time on my hands. I want to know what to do next.'

'And you need Mike for that, do you?'

'Yes,' said Eugene. 'In a word, yes.'

'Then you're going to have to learn to do otherwise,' said Margaret, 'because you can't depend on Mike to see you through. You can't depend on Mike for anything — you should know that by now.'

'But he's always helped me before.'

'Only because it suited him, and you helped him as much as he helped you.'

'But what will he do next?' asked Eugene. 'I keep thinking he's going to run off and do something new, something that doesn't need my help, and then where will that leave me?'

'Eugene, I've spent my entire married life feeling that way about Mike. And now, if he's finally decided to do it – if he's finally decided to bugger off and leave us on our own – well, you couldn't blame him, could you? There's neither of us exactly blame-free where Mike is concerned.'

'Does he know about us?'

'There is no us, Eugene; I've told you that. There's one mistake, that's all; one mistake that I'm going to pay the price of forever, that's all – a mistake.'

The millennium, thought Margaret. The fucking millennium – there were so many high expectations over such a big nothing, over the passing of time only. They were trying to be realistic about it and had decided to celebrate it at home alone – or at home alone with Eugene. His relationship with his girlfriend hadn't worked out and he'd spent most of the nineties on his own. He was now determinedly single. Margaret had the impression he'd been badly hurt and wasn't going to go there again, like a research project that had gone horribly wrong. Margaret didn't mind letting the millennium pass in this way – there was a little bit of symmetry in both starting and ending the decade with the three of them celebrating in the house together.

Only that wasn't quite how it worked out. Mike, being Mike, decided he had to be some place else at the last minute. One of their clients was jittery over the millennium and Mike volunteered to be on site to make sure nothing went wrong come the stroke of midnight. Eugene assured him everything would be fine and Mike knew that it would, but he said that wasn't the point –

it was a question of reassuring their client, showing how much they cared and keeping the contract for another thousand years.

After midnight, once the kids had gone to bed – Jack was out all night at a friend's party – Margaret and Eugene had rolled themselves a joint and waited for Mike to come home. And waited. They were huddled together on the sofa, Eugene's arm around Margaret. There was nothing unusual in this but there was in what Margaret did next – turning to kiss Eugene and lifting herself across him. They had a hasty, fumbling fuck, their minds hazy with the dope and listening out for the sounds of Mike returning and the kids upstairs. It was Margaret who led Eugene but he didn't need much persuading. She was glad; it felt good, both the sex and the lesson she was giving Mike. She got her own back that night – for all the absences and for all the secrets – a pre-emptive strike for all the times to come.

Eugene had left before Mike came home soon after two o'clock. Margaret had showered and was in her bed.

The millennium, she thought, the fucking millennium.

Margaret picked up her bag off the kitchen table.

'Mike wouldn't just leave,' said Eugene. 'He wouldn't just go without saying anything.'

'You don't know what Mike might do,' said Margaret. 'I don't know what Mike might do. I don't even know if he's really gone to Dublin, though from the look on your face I suspect he has. But I don't know why.'

'He couldn't just leave,' said Eugene, 'not with . . . not with everything that's happening.'

'Make up your mind, Eugene,' said Margaret. 'You just told me there's nothing happening, that there's nothing for you to do at work. If Mike's bored with his job, he'll be making plans to do something else – you can depend on that.'

'I don't mean that, Margaret, and you know it.'

Margaret put down her bag.

'What do you want, Eugene?' she asked. 'Why are you really here? And why come this morning, of all mornings, when you know Mike won't be around? What were you doing, waiting out in the street for me to come home alone?'

'That's not fair – '

'Why is it that you only ever call when you know I'll be here on my own?'

'Margaret – '

'Is this it?' she asked. Margaret pushed her right hand to her breast, and felt herself through the silk of her blouse.

'Margaret – '

'Is this it?' She reached down to the hem of her skirt and lifted it above her waist; it was close fitting and this wasn't so easy to do. 'Is this what you came for?' She touched herself through her underwear. 'Or this?' she asked, and turned round and smacked her arse. 'Come on, Eugene, at least be honest with yourself. It's here for you if you want it.' Margaret slapped herself again, but when Eugene didn't move she felt ridiculous and pulled her skirt back down. When she saw the look on Eugene's face she knew she'd hurt him, but that was what she'd wanted to do.

Eugene turned to go, but then he hesitated. 'Margaret,' he said, 'you and Mike are my best friends.'

'Your only friends, you mean.'

'No, actually, you're not my only friends. But you are my best friends and I care about you, whether you want me to or not.'

'We don't need your pity, Eugene.'

'It's not pity, Margaret. You can't ignore what's going on here, and falling out with Mike isn't going to help.'

'Maybe we should have thought of that before.'

'For fuck's sake, Margaret! I'm not talking about that, and you know it.'

'So what are you talking about?'

'I . . . I know I've made things worse in the past – '

'No, you haven't, Eugene,' said Margaret. 'I enjoyed our little fuck that time, our little fuck to see in the new millennium.'

'Margaret – '

'Stop saying my fucking name, can't you?'

'If there's anything . . . if there's anything I can do to help you, then please just say, but, Margaret, you've got to face up to what's happening – you and Mike both.'

'You can help, Eugene,' said Margaret.

'Yes?'

'You can help by not calling around here when you know Mike's away. That would be a start.'

'Margaret, I – '

'And then you can help by fucking off and getting your own life and not being so dependent on Mike all the time and now I'd like you to just leave.'

'Margaret,' said Eugene, 'I know this is hard, and I understand if you want to take it out on me – God knows I've got it coming. And I won't call again if that's what you want – '

'That's what I want!' said Margaret.

'Are you even going to the hospital today?' asked Eugene. 'You have to at least go visit her, Margaret.'

'I told you I wasn't working at the hospital today.'

'That's not what I – Margaret, you have to face up to what's happening.' Eugene knew he was repeating himself, but he couldn't think of any other way to put it – this was what he'd come to say.

'I don't have to do anything,' said Margaret.

'But she's your daughter, for Christ's sake.'

'I want you to leave now.'

'Please, Margaret.'

'Please, Eugene,' she mimicked. 'Just go, will you – now?'

Margaret lifted the strap of her bag across her shoulder and turned away from Eugene. She heard him leave the kitchen, walk down the hallway and out the front door. Only then did she allow herself to breathe. She tried to think what else she might need for the rest of the day. She gave herself a few more minutes, and then picked up her car keys. She left the kitchen and closed the door behind her. At the front door she couldn't resist checking that Eugene really had left, but his car was gone. She locked the door behind her and walked to her car.

Margaret drove to Withington for her two o'clock. She was in good time, but she needed that time to compose herself for the session. She waited in the car rather than go in a cafe for some lunch. The session went okay – a lot easier than the morning out at Alderley Edge. Margaret suspected this had something to do with her having less sympathy for the woman she was counselling, and this allowed her to be more dispassionate in her handling of the case. But this gave Margaret cause for concern that how she responded to a person should have a bearing on her ability to counsel them. Once again, she made a mental note to include a query in her written notes later in the day.

The temptation was there to have a little snooze in the car afterwards, but Margaret resisted it and drove back through Chorlton to Stretford. Driving through city streets was a very different experience to the morning's drive on the motorway, and Margaret stayed alert for the short journey. She passed by the entrance to her road on the way to the crisis centre in Stretford, but Margaret decided not to call in at home. She was early for her hour's shift, and the manager of the centre commented on how keen she must be. Calls came in, but none were put through to Margaret and she was able to get on with writing up her notes on the day's sessions. Margaret asked the manager if it was okay to continue into the next hour – she could be available to take calls while working on her project – but surprisingly the manager refused.

'I think you should go home,' she told Margaret. 'You don't look too well.'

'No, I'm fine,' said Margaret. 'I just need a cup of tea. I forgot to have lunch today, that's all.'

'Still,' said the manager, 'I think you've done enough for today.'

Margaret almost pointed out that she'd not actually taken any calls for the whole of her shift, but then she realized this might have been deliberately arranged by the manager. Embarrassed, she made a show of checking the rota for her next shift, and then said her goodbyes.

'Get some rest,' said the manager as Margaret left the building. 'You look all in.'

Margaret sat in her car and switched on the engine. She didn't want to go back to an empty house, but there was nowhere else to go. Now that it was later in the day and people were returning from work, it was harder to find parking close to the house; Margaret had to double back to a space she'd seen at the entrance to the road. She checked for Eugene's car as she drove by the house, but it wasn't there.

Margaret sat for a long time in the car. She was mortified at what they apparently thought of her at the centre. Was it so obvious that something was wrong at home? Did everybody know? Did she only volunteer as a substitute for confronting her own problems? And the counselling – was she really so suited to counselling if she allowed her emotions to interfere with her handling of a case? Margaret was a good nurse, she knew she was. So why couldn't she get the balance right in this – that all-important balance between professional concern and competence?

Margaret spent her days being there for other people, but her own life was falling apart. She sat in her car and watched the traffic pass by along the main road. People were going home for the evening, to their families, to their partners and to their children. Her own empty house was behind her, but it was no longer a home.

She was so ashamed. She was ashamed of who she had become, and she was ashamed of the way she'd humiliated Eugene. She had humiliated herself.

Margaret took out her mobile phone and checked it for messages; there were none.

Where was Mike?

She dropped the phone back into her bag. She knew she had no option but to go into the house alone. She picked up her bag, got out of the car and pressed the remote. She walked back along the street and up the steps to her front door. She went inside and closed the door behind her. She stood with her back to the door and listened to the silence of the house. She looked at the telephone in the hallway.

She picked up the receiver and dialled Mike's

mobile number, but her call went straight through to his message system. She hung up before saying anything.

Maybe Mike was on his way home?

Margaret picked up the phone and dialled again.

'Mike . . .' she said, but that was all. She didn't know what else to say. Tell him she loved him? That she wished he were home? That he was coming home?

Was he coming home? Was he ever coming home?

Margaret ran out of time before she could say anything else and she didn't phone again. She dialled Eugene's home number but when it rang out a few times she knew that this, too, was going on to a message.

'Eugene,' she said, 'it's Margaret. Please pick up the phone.'

Nothing.

'I'm so sorry for this morning,' she said. 'I know . . . I know you probably can't, but, please, if you're there, pick up the phone.'

She waited but there was nothing, and then the line went dead. Margaret continued to speak into the receiver.

'I'm so ashamed,' she said. 'I'm so ashamed, Eugene – of us, and of everything.'

But when Margaret put down the phone and stood alone in her hallway she knew it wasn't Eugene she had to talk to – it wasn't even her husband Mike. She couldn't confide in her boys, because Jack and Mike junior were gone. It was healthy that they were gone, but Margaret missed them all the same; she missed the strength they'd so often given her in the past.

She knew what she had to do for this mess to be made right again. She knew what she had to do. She just didn't think she had the courage to do it.

5

It was past two o'clock by the time Mike had persuaded Katie to come back with him to Manchester. He'd bought tickets for several flights throughout the early evening, all business class, and a return for Katie on the last flight back to Dublin at nine o'clock. Mike was delighted that Katie had her passport; he'd been prepared to wait while she went home to fetch it. He was prepared to do anything to make this happen.

'You've some nerve booking me a flight,' said Katie.

'It's only money,' replied Mike. 'There was every chance you might not agree to see me, remember?'

Katie didn't know what Mike hoped she could achieve but since she wasn't about to return to work for the afternoon, she thought she might as well give him the rest of the day. It didn't matter to Katie if a few hours of that day were spent flying back and forth across the Irish Sea; it was only the fact that it was Manchester that unnerved her.

'If we leave now,' said Mike, 'we might catch a flight at four o'clock.'

Mike walked across to the reception desk to settle his bill, though, from what Katie could see, he'd only used the bar.

Katie didn't like the idea of interfering in Mike's

family, but he assured her they wouldn't be disturbed. Official visiting hours at the hospital weren't until seven o'clock, and the unspoken implication was that nobody would be there to visit Katherine anyway.

'You won't even know you're there,' said Mike. 'She's in Wythenshawe Hospital, right next to the airport.'

'I know where Wythenshawe Hospital is,' said Katie. She felt tetchy – it was a long time since she'd been home. She'd kept herself ready for over twenty years to leave at a moment's notice, but she wasn't too happy now that moment had come that it was Manchester she was running to.

They didn't talk much on the journey over; there was little more to be said and Mike knew better than to expect any small talk from Katie.

The plane flew in over south Manchester.

'Where are you from, Katie?' asked Mike.

'You mean where was I born, and where did I live, and all that?'

'Yes,' said Mike, 'all the normal things.'

'Gorton,' said Katie. 'I'm from Gorton.'

'That's over by Ashton, isn't it?'

'Yes,' said Katie, 'around there.'

'So we'll have passed nearby when we used to drive out to the hills?'

'Not really,' said Katie. 'That was closer to Oldham than Ashton.'

Even so, Mike sat on the plane and thought of Katie back then – how she was so close to her home and never said a word.

But this was all Mike got out of Katie. He'd never know that Katie had had a whole different childhood – if you could call it that – before she was taken into care in Gorton. He'd never learn how she came to be living in Hulme and studying law by the time she was twenty. He'd never know because he'd never ask, and he'd never ask because he knew she'd never tell.

Katie and Mike had eaten on the plane. The food was good and helped fill the silence between them. The stewardess cleared away their drinks glasses for landing.

If Katie thought of anything, it was to question the sense in Mike asking her to come. Who in his right mind would let another headcase like Katie within a million miles of his daughter? But then, maybe that was it – none of them were in their right minds here. If this was what Mike wanted, if this was what he was asking of Katie, then so be it. She would try to help; and she'd make every effort not to do Katherine any further harm. Now Katie was here, she would do what was asked of her, but she couldn't help but be concerned about what the next two hours might bring.

They had no baggage, so they were quickly through to arrivals and then out to the car park.

'Do you ever worry that you might be stopped at customs one day?' asked Katie.

'As in properly stopped?' asked Mike. 'For all my past sins, you mean?'

'Yes,' said Katie. 'That they might be looking for you, or at least looking to stop you coming back into the country?'

'Well, obviously it's occurred to me otherwise I'd never have come up with that story this morning, but no, I don't live in fear of the past.'

'Have you been back to the States since?'

'No,' said Mike. 'I don't want to push my luck. I think it was a good plan at the time, and I think we got away with it, but I don't like the idea of Bruno still being out there somewhere.'

'As a loose end, you mean?'

'Yes,' said Mike. 'It's a shame to say it, but that's how I think of Bruno now – as a messy loose end that might come back to haunt me. I gave up worrying about him a long time ago, though; I've bigger things to worry about now. This is us, here,' he said.

'You got rid of the Jag, then?' said Katie, once they were in the car.

Mike reversed out of the parking space.

'It's going to take more than driving a Volvo to keep my family safe,' he said.

They drove straight to the hospital. Mike had to brake hard twice to avoid other cars as he searched for a space in the hospital car park.

'Are you sure about this?' asked Katie. She looked across at Mike; he was becoming increasingly agitated and less and less like Mike.

'No,' he said. 'No, I'm not sure.'

'I don't know what I'm doing here,' said Katie.

'It made sense when I set out to ask you this morning.'

261

'I don't know what you hope I can do.'

'Talk to her,' said Mike. 'That's all – just talk to her.'

They walked from the car park to the hospital entrance. The complex of buildings was confusing and Katie let Mike lead the way. Inside, there was a large expanse of floor with a reception desk in the middle.

'If you wait here,' said Mike, 'I'll just make sure that it's okay to go in before visiting hours.'

Katie sat down to one side on one of the many plastic chairs placed around the entrance hall. She suspected Mike had gone to check on Katherine and not on the visiting hours; she wondered what would happen if she was too ill to be seen.

'Come on,' said Mike, when he returned. His face was drained of its usual freshness and youth.

He looks like an old man, Katie thought for the first time.

They walked down a long corridor, one side of which faced on to an inner courtyard. Then they turned into a ward of private rooms. Mike opened a door and stood back to allow Katie through. He gestured with his hand – part invitation and part introduction.

Katie could see that Mike was in bits. She took a hold of his hand. So many years between them and so little physical contact – it was strange to touch the skin of a man she knew so well and yet barely knew at all.

'You'd better leave us alone,' she said.

Mike looked across the room, from Katie to his daughter on the bed, and then looked back down at the ground.

'Please, Mike,' said Katie. 'And don't wait around here; wait outside the ward, or at the entrance where we came into the hospital.'

Mike hesitated, and then nodded in agreement. He reached up to Katie's face with his free hand, but she moved away from his touch.

'Go on,' she said. 'I'll find you when I'm through.'

She pushed him away and pulled the door across to shut him out. She didn't know what she could possibly do here, but she knew Mike had to be elsewhere.

As soon as Mike had left, Katie realized this had come too quickly; she hadn't thought it through. But if she had, would she have come? Hearing Mike, seeing Mike, could she have refused this request? Could she ever refuse Mike anything? Probably not.

Katie closed the door. She looked through the glass and watched as Mike walked away down the corridor.

She waited a second or so, and then turned into the room. She looked across at the figure on the bed. Was Katherine conscious, or aware? Might she have witnessed the intimacy between Katie and Mike? According to Mike, the doctors believed Katherine was going in and out of consciousness.

Katie rested her weight on the handle of the door. Now that she was here, Katie felt certain that Katherine was a conscious presence in the room. She had to believe this, otherwise there really was no point.

The room was nice, but Katie guessed this was the point of paying for a private room – no public ward hell for Mike Maguire's daughter. There were flowers on every available surface, and cards and some stuffed toys. The wear and tear on the toys suggested they belonged to Katherine, playthings from a childhood that was not so very long ago. No amount of flowers or cards or toys could distract Katie from the real business of the room, however. Katherine lay on the bed flanked by monitors and support machines and, suspended above her, the drip that fed into her arm.

Katie pushed herself away from the door and into the room. All the machinery was around the head of the bed and along the far side of Katherine. Katie picked up a chair and carried it to the near side of the bed. She breathed deeply and looked down at Katherine.

Oh fuck, she thought, what are you doing to yourself?

'Katherine.'

Katie said the name out loud, to see how it sounded on her tongue. She didn't expect a reply. She held on to the back of the chair and traced the metal studs that pinned down the leather upholstery. She forced herself to look at Katherine's face – it was a hard face to look at.

The lack of a reply accentuated the buzz and hum of the support machines. How quiet it would seem if they just turned everything off.

'I don't know if you can hear me,' she said, 'or even if you know that I'm here.'

This is the last thing you need, Katie thought for Katherine.

And this is the last thing you need, she thought for herself.

Katie took off her coat and laid it across the back of the chair, but she didn't sit down. She introduced herself and tried to explain how Mike had asked her to come visit, but it was hopeless. She was a stranger here.

'I'm sorry,' she said. 'This is really hard.'

She thought about leaving the room and going back out to Mike. But she stayed.

Just talk, thought Katie. Just talk. She came out with what felt like short bursts of words, followed by longer periods of silence – a silence that was really the humming noise of the machines. It was a strange and exhausting experience to try to communicate with someone in this way.

She talked about her years with Mike and this made her think of the years without – twenty years was a long time for her to have been on her own.

'Your dad just let me be me,' she said. 'He just let me be me.'

Katie was still standing by the chair. She inclined her head slightly, as if asking Katherine for permission to sit down – and then decided to sit anyway. It felt more intimate to be down on the chair. Katherine's left hand – her free hand away from all the instruments – was on the bed covers, close to where Katie sat. An identification bracelet was around her wrist.

'Your dad was in love with me back then,' said Katie.

She watched for some reaction, but there was nothing. This wasn't getting any easier.

'Your dad was in love with me, but I couldn't love him back. It wasn't that I couldn't love him; it was just that I couldn't love anybody . . . in that way.'

Christ, thought Katie, what does she need to know this for? What good can it do? You only have one shot at this so don't fuck it up.

'Your dad accepted that he could never understand me,' she said. 'I gave him nothing, and he accepted it. I never gave him an explanation and he never asked me for one and that's why I still owe him, even after all these years.

'I'm not sure I fully appreciated what your dad did for me at the time, but I do now.'

Katie stopped and put her head in her hands. This was unreal – talking into silence. Every now and again she'd get the feeling that Katherine was listening, at least to the sound of her voice, but surely this was a mistaken hope? What would Katie's voice mean to Katherine anyway? It was going to take more than this to bring her back.

Katie looked at Katherine on the bed. There was a clock on one of the monitors. It was almost seven o'clock – the official visiting time was about to begin. Katie had been in the room for almost an hour; she was beginning to appreciate Katherine's stubborn refusal to do anything but breathe.

Katie stood up and walked to the door. She rested her hand on the door and took a deep breath – a very different breath to the short, snatched gasps of Katherine on the bed behind her. She looked through the glass door out into the corridor.

What was she doing here? This was wasting everybody's time.

Katie turned again towards the room. She walked over to pick up one of the stuffed toys from the shelf. It was a purple teddy bear, soft and homely, and Katie knew it would be Katherine's favourite – it was a colour thing. She replaced the teddy on the shelf and returned to her seat.

She wondered if Katherine had any control left over her body. At what point would Katherine's own strong will, her determination to hurt her parents for hurting her, give way to a body that could no longer help itself? Katherine's strength of mind was making her body weaker.

There's something to admire in all of this, thought Katie.

'I told you those things about your dad,' she said, 'because I want you to know that I understand what it means to be loved by him. I don't think for one minute that I can change your mind here, but I want you to know this isn't the first time your dad has failed to understand a person he loves. It's not the first time he's been unable to help someone who needs his help – and he hates it.'

Katie thought for a while.

'But this won't make any difference to you, will it? I mean, nothing I say will change the way you feel; I know you won't let yourself be helped. But the thing is – whatever you decide to do – your dad's going to love you anyway. Even if you hurt him like this, he'll still love you. I know, because he did the same for me, and he got nothing from me but pain – well, maybe we had some fun – but still all he did was love me and set me free.'

Again Katie was quiet for a long time.

'And then he made his life with your mother and he had you, his children. And I guess there were good times and bad times, like there are in any family, but nothing prepared him for this – except me, maybe, and I think that's why I'm here . . .

'He'd try anything rather than lose you.

'But I think it might be too late.'

Katie leant forward over the bed and tentatively touched Katherine's left hand lying palm down on the bed covers. At Katie's touch, Katherine's hand moved slightly – a short, spasmodic response. Katie took her hand away and looked at Katherine. She reached again so that the tips of Katherine's fingers were rested on her own. There was no substance there, no weight. Katie stroked the fingers with her thumb.

'When your dad asked me to come here,' she said, 'I think he thought I might be the only person who could understand you. And that if I could understand you, I might be able to persuade you to change your mind. Or that I'd be able to tell you something about myself that would make you feel you weren't so alone, that you weren't so uniquely on your own.

'He's right about me, but I think he's wrong about what I can do for you. No one can help you but yourself, and if you don't want to help yourself, then that's an end to it. And it's an end to you.'

Katie took a deep breath.

'If you can hear me, Katherine, if you can hear me and you want to listen, then this is what I want to say.

'Don't live your life like me. I found a way through, but it's not much of a way. I think it's a coward's way compared to what you're doing.

'I could tell you all about myself, but I don't think it would mean anything. I think you'd say it has nothing to do with you . . .

'And you'd be right.

'I could tell you about myself, but I can't remember most of what there is to tell.'

Katie could remember a woman holding her face between her hands, but she could only guess who that woman was.

'And isn't that the point? That we're like we are for reasons we don't want to remember?

'So, no, Katherine,' she said. 'Don't live your life like me. I love your dad. I've always loved him, and I think I always will, but I'll never be with him because I can't let myself . . . I can't let myself and it's so crap – it's just so crap, so, please, don't ever be like me.

'I wish you could hear me. Whatever it is that's wrong, I know you think there's nothing that can put it right. It's just that, well, it's just that if I had the choice again,

269

then . . . I don't know. Twenty years spent on my own when someone could have loved me, if only I'd let him. Twenty years when someone might have allowed me to be me – when someone who didn't know what it was they were offering but was prepared to offer it anyway – maybe that was too good a thing to pass up on.

'And for what – so I could be on my own?

'For a reason I can't remember?

'Not much of a trade, really; not much of an invest-ment.'

There was a drop of moisture between the tips of Katie's and Katherine's fingers. Katie took away her hand and wiped her fingers on the bedclothes.

'I think you should do what's right for you,' she said. 'And if this is what's right for you, then this is what you should do. But I wish it wasn't. I wish you could get well – for yourself and for your dad and for your brothers – and for your mum. I wish we could get to meet and talk properly; I could tell you some things. I'd like to get to know the daughter of Nice Guy Mike, because if things had been different, she might have been my daughter too.

'I wish you could get well to see that this isn't all there is, that there'll be other days, better days.

'But I think I'm too late, and I'm sorry.'

Katie stood up. She leant into Katherine's face and put her lips to Katherine's cheek.

'Goodbye,' she said.

Katie pulled away and stood up. She picked up her

coat, returned the chair to the back wall and left the room. As she walked down the corridor her balance gave way. She leant on a handrail running along the length of the wall, and stopped for a second before recovering and walking on. She found her way to the hospital entrance and saw Mike, sat with his arms crossed and his legs outstretched on the far side of the hallway.

As he saw Katie approach, Mike unfolded his arms and sat up in the chair. He looked up at her.

'I'm so sorry, Mike,' she said. 'I'm so sorry.'

She sat down on the hard plastic chair next to him.

What could she say? Nothing, so she said nothing at all.

They sat like this, together in silence, for almost five minutes.

'Will you stay in touch, do you think?' asked Mike eventually.

'I don't know,' said Katie. 'Whether that would be such a good idea or not, I mean.'

'Have you a phone number I can contact you on?' asked Mike. 'A home number, or a mobile?'

'I don't have a mobile,' said Katie, 'and I think I'd rather contact you, if that's okay? I know I can't stop you phoning me at work, but I'd prefer it if you didn't.'

'You're going to disappear again, aren't you?'

'Not necessarily, no,' said Katie. 'Give me your mobile number; I'll need to know about Katherine, at the very least.'

She took out a pen and a small black address book from her bag.

'Do you have many names listed in there?' asked Mike.

'Not so many, really,' she said. 'Go on, what's your number?'

She wrote it down, and put the pen and book away in her bag. It was time for her to leave.

'I'm going to take a cab to the airport,' she said.

'I don't mind running you there,' said Mike, but they both knew he should go back in to Katherine.

'I'll need some of your quaint English money, though,' said Katherine.

Mike took out his wallet and handed Katie a tenner.

Four nurses walked past, talking loudly, about to start their shift on the wards. Katie watched Mike watch them go by. The entrance hall was busy with friends and families visiting for the hour between seven and eight. Lots of questions were being asked at reception and directions given. Katie looked at the faces – some were tired, some were worried and some were relieved. Some, Katie could see, were overjoyed; people did get well here – that was the point of a hospital, right?

'What am I going to do?' asked Mike.

'Go back in to your daughter,' said Katie. 'And trust that your love pulls her through.'

'And if it doesn't?'

'That's not trusting, Mike; you have to believe it will. I think . . .'

Katie hesitated before coming out with any inane platitudes.

'She's very sick, Mike,' she said, 'and I'm not sure there's much you can do if Katherine doesn't want to get better. I wish I could have come here and waved my magic wand, but I think you knew that wouldn't happen. If the doctors can't help her, I don't see how I can. But I'm glad you brought me over.'

'I just feel so fucking useless,' said Mike.

'I know, I know,' said Katie. 'But you do have the one thing that can help Katherine – you love your daughter. So go back in there and stay with her, and don't leave her until she's better; it's all you can do.'

Mike looked up and across to the exit door of the hospital, not seeing much through his tears.

'I don't want to lose contact with you again,' he said. 'I miss you; I miss having you around.'

Katie didn't reply immediately.

'I don't know, Mike,' she said. 'This is difficult for me. Let me think about it, but I promise you I'll call. It's just that – '

'You can't promise anything else for now?'

'That's about how it is,' said Katie.

She stood to go.

'You're always leaving me,' said Mike.

'I know,' said Katie. 'It's what I do.'

She reached down and touched the side of Mike's face.

'Don't give up hope,' said Katie. 'You're all she has, and she's going to need you.'

She turned and walked away towards the exit. Somebody called out to her across the floor. 'Katie.'

She looked up and saw Eugene; she recognized him immediately.

'Eugene,' she said.

He blushed. He wasn't alone, but he left the woman he was with and walked over to where Katie waited by the door.

'I wondered why Mike wanted to see you again,' he said.

'Is that who I think it is?' asked Katie.

Eugene looked back to where Margaret waited in the middle of the entrance hall.

'Yes,' he said.

'She's tiny,' said Katie.

'She's tiny, but tough – I hope,' said Eugene. 'Does this mean Mike's in the hospital?'

Did Mike's presence make this visit easier for Eugene, or harder? Katie didn't know.

'He's over there,' she said.

Mike had seen the three of them across the hallway and was about to come over. It was time for Katie to leave.

'Eugene,' called Margaret.

Katie could see that Margaret was in some distress.

'Can you wait for me?' Eugene asked Katie.

'I have a plane to catch,' she said.

'I could drive you to the airport,' he suggested.

'I don't think so,' said Katie.

'Eugene,' called Margaret again.

It wasn't fair to leave Eugene like this, but there was enough going on without Katie coming face to face with Margaret – it might undo everything.

'I have Mike's number,' she said to Eugene. 'I'll be in touch.'

'Will you?' he asked.

'Yes,' said Katie. 'Yes.'

She walked away. She knew she was being rude, but it was the right thing to do.

Outside, Katie saw the last cab pull away from the rank. She guessed there'd be another one on the way. She walked over to the rank and waited.

'Come on,' she said. 'Come on.'

She had to get away from here. She watched as a cab arrived at the entrance to the hospital and dropped off a passenger – a woman, alone. The cab doubled back and drove up to where Katie waited.

'The airport, please,' she said, and the cab pulled away.

Katie enjoyed travelling on her own, and the journey home to Dublin was easy. The short trips from the airport to Wythenshawe Hospital and back again to the airport meant something to Katie. It was her first time in Manchester for over twenty years. Nothing much had changed – newer roads, maybe, but that was all. It was a place like any other, and Katie's world hadn't stopped. She felt strong enough to maybe arrange a longer visit next time; to face up to whatever memories the city might hold for her.

It might be nice to try again – to be amongst friends like Eugene, and Mike maybe, if that was possible. Despite herself, Katie had friends – Carmel at work, for example – and she didn't have to be as alone as she'd chosen to be.

Katie hoped she might get to know Katherine one day. It was unlikely, even if Katherine were to get well, but not impossible. Whatever chance Katherine had of recovering was with her parents' help, and it looked as though Eugene was working to make that happen.

Pleasant thoughts like these made the journey pass quickly for Katie; thinking was one of the joys of travelling on her own. Perhaps the time was right to start planning a more serious journey, to rediscover the travel bug she'd lost over the past few years? Katie needed to loosen up a little; she was in danger of becoming stale if she didn't.

Nothing much had changed in Dublin either: there was still no rail link from the airport to the city. Katie took a cab to Killester Station, and caught the DART home to Monkstown. The track curved around the bay, with the dark of the sea on one side and the lights of the city on the other. It could have been beautiful, but it wasn't. Katie sat in the bright carriage and thought about Dublin. It was obviously time for her to move on – start again some place else – but where could she go, and what could she do? Financially, anything was possible, but Katie wanted a life, a proper life, and not just this pretence of living.

She knew that no amount of yoga was ever going

to rid her mind of Bruno, and no matter what she did to herself, she'd never cut away what had happened to her as a child. She'd always be the same Katie McGuire – there were some things she couldn't change – but that wasn't so bad, was it?

The train arrived at Monkstown. Katie walked up from the station to her home; she'd call Mike in the morning.

Acknowledgements

I'd like to thank Andrew Davies for the bits he allowed me to steal from his book *B Monkey* – including my title.

He just wanted a decent book to read ...

Not too much to ask, is it? It was in 1935 when Allen Lane, Managing Director of Bodley Head Publishers, stood on a platform at Exeter railway station looking for something good to read on his journey back to London. His choice was limited to popular magazines and poor-quality paperbacks – the same choice faced every day by the vast majority of readers, few of whom could afford hardbacks. Lane's disappointment and subsequent anger at the range of books generally available led him to found a company – and change the world.

'We believed in the existence in this country of a vast reading public for intelligent books at a low price, and staked everything on it'
Sir Allen Lane, 1902–1970, founder of Penguin Books

The quality paperback had arrived – and not just in bookshops. Lane was adamant that his Penguins should appear in chain stores and tobacconists, and should cost no more than a packet of cigarettes.

Reading habits (and cigarette prices) have changed since 1935, but Penguin still believes in publishing the best books for everybody to enjoy. We still believe that good design costs no more than bad design, and we still believe that quality books published passionately and responsibly make the world a better place.

So wherever you see the little bird – whether it's on a piece of prize-winning literary fiction or a celebrity autobiography, political tour de force or historical masterpiece, a serial-killer thriller, reference book, world classic or a piece of pure escapism – you can bet that it represents the very best that the genre has to offer.

Whatever you like to read – trust Penguin.